Dr. Strangelove

Film Ink Series

★ for copyright reasons these titles are not available in the USA or Canada in the Prion edition.

DR. STRANGELOVE
OR HOW I LEARNED TO STOP
WORRYING AND LOVE THE BOMB

Peter George

This edition published in 2000 by
Prion Books Limited
Imperial Works, Perren Street,
London NW5 3ED

Reprinted 2001

ISBN-1-85375-310-6

Cover design by Bob Eames
Printed and bound in Great Britain by
Bookmarque Limited, Croydon, Surrey

Publisher's Note

The pages which make up this bizarre and ancient comedy were discovered at the bottom of a deep crevice in the Great Northern Desert of planet Earth. The reader will see that there is a short introduction written by the men who discovered the manuscript. Aside from this, the pages are presented in exactly the form in which they were found. After the end of the story there is also a brief epilogue which states why we have published this book.

introduction

The story opens during the latter half of Earth's twentieth century. We do not know quite why this dating system was used, since we have evidence of life on Earth long before this. But we assume that after some unprecedented disaster it was agreed by the survivors to start a fresh count on time. This has mainly been our experience in other worlds.

At this stage the technology of Earth, though still crude by our standards, had advanced sufficiently so men had been able to build tiny thermonuclear weapons, the largest of which was only about a hundred megatons in explosive yield. But to compensate for this they had built plenty of them, enough we estimate to have destroyed the world three and a half times. Why they would have wanted to be able to do it more than once is a mystery to us.

Simple nuclear weapons had been used twice some years previously to end what men quaintly referred to as World War Two. Since then they had multiplied both in size and number. Two major powers shared between them about ninety-five per cent of this nuclear capability, both in weapons and means of delivery. They were not on friendly terms, and we find this difficult to understand, because both were governed by power systems which seem to us basically similar.

Both these major nations spent vast sums of money in competing with each other on these toys, and yet more vast sums on trying to conceal from the other their progress. One such project began about thirteen months before our story opens. Soviet scientists and engineers, backed by a great mass of volunteer labor, started work at the base of a perpetually fog-shrouded mountain in the empty arctic wasteland of northern Siberia.

In spite of the most stringent security measures, some rumors concerning the project did leak through to the rest of the world. But they were of so horrible and fantastic a nature that people did not, could not, take them seriously. Other more substantial rumors had it that on completion of the project, to maintain the greatest possible secrecy, all who had been concerned with the project were—to use their own strange phrase—*liquidated*.

At the time of our story every nation, and not least the two major powers, feared surprise attack and took all precautions against it. Yet we do not find any positive evidence that the full and infinite consequences of nuclear attack were appreciated by governments and their peoples.

In the period of which we write, one of the measures taken by the United States of America to guard against surprise attack was an airborne alert. (We have copied the phraseology current at the time.) This meant that they kept seventy jet bombers always in the air.

As crews tired they were relieved by replacement bombers, but never less than seventy were airborne and prepared for action. They were armed with full war loads of thermonuclear weapons.

One half of this airborne alert force on this day had left the Burpelson Air Force Base many hours before. They were one of Strategic Air Command's bomb wings. The planes of this wing were now dispersed from the Persian Gulf to the Arctic Ocean. They had in common only one geographic factor. All of them were approximately thirteen hundred miles from their assigned targets in enemy territory. They also had in common their bomb load. All of them carried two bombs, as well as certain other devices, which together gave a yield of forty megatons. Each bomber therefore carried the equivalent of forty million tons of TNT. It may be noted that this was about equivalent to fifteen times the amount of explosives dropped during World War Two, and about two and a half thousand times the force of the bomb dropped on Hiroshima.

One of the bombers, named by its crew *Leper Colony*, was approaching its Fail-Safe point. Once it reached this point it would automatically turn and head for home. This was of course a safety precaution, one of many these cautious but determined men had dreamed up to prevent any distressing little accident.

The crew of *Leper Colony* were highly trained and highly efficient men. They were specially selected. They were proud men, alert men, confident men; yet within each of them there was a slow accretion of tension and nervous strain.

They were men who could not afford to relax, for relaxation would perhaps menace the peace of the world.

As *Leper Colony* approached its Fail-Safe point, our story begins.

LEPER COLONY

Aesthetically the exterior shape of the airplane was pleasing. The swept wings gave an impression of arrow swiftness; the shining body, of brightness and cleanness; the eight great engines, of power and pure functional efficiency. Effortlessly, matter-of-factly, *Leper Colony* was putting nearly seven hundred airborne miles behind her each hour, scorning distance and reducing the globe to a few hours' flying time.

Inside the airplane the six men of the crew were looking forward now to turning at their Fail-Safe point. They would have to stick around the general area a little longer, it was true, but at least when they turned they were past the worst. These were men who had to pay the price of vigilance. Dedicated men. Their motto: *Peace is our profession.*

The layout of the bomber was essentially simple for so complex an airplane. In front sat the pilot and co-pilot. Behind them and facing to the rear were the defense-systems officer and the radar/radio officer with all their complicated, ingenious apparatus. On a lower deck were the navigator and the bombardier, each with his complicated devices at finger's touch. Below them again and a little aft was the bomb bay. Here were stored two thermonuclear bombs, each of twenty megatons yield. Most SAC crews had given affectionate names to the bombs they carried, and these names were usually chalked on the bomb itself.

In *Leper Colony* the bombs had been given female faces of a sort. Their names were *Hi-There* and *Lolita*.

In the pilot's section the plane commander, Major Kong, known to the rest of the crew as King, was munching a sandwich and idly flicking over pages of the current *Playboy* magazine. To the left of the serried banks of instruments there was a triptych of ancestral portraits with, reading from left to right, King's father, grandfather and great-grandfather appropriately scowling martial scowls, all of them decked in martial regalia of the past. King yawned and turned a page of *Playboy*. The plane moved steadily through the mesosphere on autopilot.

On King's right Captain G. A. Owens, known as "Ace," gazed steadily at the arctic sky. There was nothing in the sky to interest him, but even less in the airplane. Of the two boring alternatives, he preferred the sky. He gnawed occasionally at a large apple.

Lieutenant H. R. Dietrich, the defense-systems officer, was playing with a pack of cards. He executed an intricate accordion, was dissatisfied with it, tried again, and then proffered the cards to Lieutenant B. Goldberg, the radar/radio officer.

Goldberg raised his eyebrows slightly. It was a gesture he had been practicing for the past six months as a counter to Dietrich's manipulation of the cards, which Goldberg admitted was pretty damn slick. He permitted himself to accept a card, while at the same time conveying he was not really interested in the manipulation, however slick, of pieces of pasteboard. With an expression as deadpan as Dietrich's he slid the card face down on his desk and reached for his coffee and his book. There was an article in *Reader's Digest* more important than Dietrich and his fool tricks. He sipped his coffee luxuriously, ignoring Dietrich's increasing agitation.

On the lower deck, where the navigator and bombardier had their stations, the navigator slowly unwrapped a Hershey bar. Lieutenant Sweets Kivel intended to buy himself a confectionery store. For the present he had to stay in the Air Force because be needed money to buy the store, and this was a way of getting it. But not forever. Oh brother, no! Enough money—about another year he figured—and Sweets knew just the store he was aiming to buy. He munched the chocolate bar thoughtfully as he perused the *Confectioner's Journal*.

Alongside him the bombardier, Lieutenant Lothar Zogg, an intelligent but rather smug young Negro from New York, was pointedly staring at the navigational charts that lay ignored while Sweets read his journal. He nudged Sweets with his leg, said, "How about that turn point?"

Lieutenant Kivel laid down his journal. "Well, yeah, Lothar, okay, let's wait a minute, huh?" He clicked on his intercom. "Hey, King, three minutes to turn point; fresh heading will be three-five-three." He waited for King's acknowledgment, then sank back in his seat, conscious of a job well done. He picked up the copy of the *Confectioner's Journal* he had laid on his chart table while he called King and began to read with renewed interest.

Major King Kong watched the three minutes pass on his watch. Fifteen seconds before the time, he leaned forward, and with the easy practiced grace of the veteran pilot, turned the autopilot gyro heading to three-five-three. He watched the turning of the plane with close attention, allowing his copy of *Playboy* to fall between him and his co-pilot, Ace Owens. Ace was quick to pick up the copy, begin to turn its pages.

"Roger," King said. Even in that one word it was possible to distinguish his unmistakable Texas drawl. "Headin' three-five-three."

Ace Owens examined the photo fold-out of "Playmate of the Month." He contemplated the photo with reverence, almost awe, then he said, "Miss Foreign Affairs...thirty-eight...twenty-four...thirty-six, and a top-rated Washington secretary. How about that, King?"

King frowned, made sure that the plane had rounded out of the turn, locked the gyros, then said judicially, "How about what, Ace? Great statistics. Great secretary. Prob'ly holds the world's horizontal shorthand record. But what else, Ace?"

Ace looked at the photo again. He said, "King, you know she kind of reminds me of that brunette I, I mean you, I mean we, had back in Houston, you remember? What the hell was her name?"

"Hold up the photo, Ace. Give ole King a good, long look. Yeah, you're right, son. You're right. Name of Mary Ellen." He paused for a moment, looking at the foldout in detail. "Yeah, reckon you might draw one or two comparisons at that."

"She was a doll. A real live doll."

"Prime cut and double grade-A premium," King assented. "Ain't seen me with no other kind, have you, boy?"

"No," Owens said, "guess I haven't ever, King. You know, you had it so good so long I don't think you even appreciate it any more."

"Well now," King said. "Me, I'd question that. 'Preciate it? Hell, me an' ole Bull Daddy got one whole oil well down in San Anton' just to show our 'preciation."

"You mean Bull Daddy he's still at it?"

"Hell yes," King said with quiet pride. "*And* I reckon ole Bull Daddy's aimin' to be top gun in our outfit for a while yet."

"But he must be pushing seventy-five, King."

King lit a cigar with care. He made sure it was drawing satisfactorily, inhaled luxuriously, then said, "Seventy-five nothin'. That horny ole bastard's seventy-eight next month. Lemme tell you, Ace, ole Bull Daddy jest wrote me a letter about this little ole gal he had come down from Pecos. Seems he turned that gal every way but loose." King leaned back on his seat, raised his legs so his half riding boots rested on the instrument panel in front of him, and gave vent to a rebel *Gee-haw* that echoed through the airplane. The crew ignored it. They were accustomed to King. And of course they had their own cards, magazines, journals, and books to occupy them.

"But ole Bull Daddy he's a damn fool about some things. Not that I'd be right anxious to inform him about that, you understand, but the fact is, number one, he's a romantic fool when it comes to foolin' around with women, and number two, he ain't got no *taste*. He used to say, 'Why hell, boy, you just throw a gunny sack over their heads and you can't tell one from the other.'"

Once again King's rebel yell was heard in the plane. Then he went on, "And he's tied onto some real dogs too, I'll tell you that. But not me, ole buddy. I've got to have it prime cut and double grade-A premium."

Ace Owens shook his head admiringly. "Yeah, King," he said, "you're lucky. *You* got taste."

"Yeah, I guess I do, an' I guess I'm lucky about a lot of things. I mean, you name it an' I've had it. Prime cut right off the top hindquarter. But all kiddin' aside, Ace, there's one thing in this ole world don't have no price tag on. An' money sure ain't done me no good there. It's somethin' leaves a man, well, kind of incomplete without it."

Ace Owens looked at King curiously. He could not

imagine any way in which King's life had been incomplete. He said, "What's that, King?"

"It's one thing I never had an' I don't guess I ever will have now. *Combat!*"

Lieutenant Dietrich, the defense-systems officer, reluctantly put down the pack of cards he had been manipulating as an electronic sound alarm directed his attention to one of his radarscopes. Dietrich had several of these scopes banked in front of him, but the alarm he had heard was connected to the maximum range search radar. He made a minor adjustment to the tuning of the set, then moved a strobe marker to the blip that had appeared at the outer rim of the scope. He read off the range of the object, then said through the intercom, his voice undisturbed and reporting a routine occurrence, "Bogey at one-four-five, approximately a hundred and thirty-five miles."

Sweets Kivel, the navigator, carefully turned over his copy of the *Confectioner's Journal* so as not to lose his place and quickly plotted the position of the bogey on his chart.

King, who had been musing sadly about the one thing lacking in his life, said casually, "Probably one of their radar surveillance jobs."

On Dietrich's scope the blip suddenly vanished as segments of the scope became obscured by brilliant light. Owens said, "He jammed us out. Showing off his ECM. What a jerk!"

Ace Owens, who had taken up the copy of *Playboy* again, said absently, "I wonder just why he's doing that?"

Dietrich came in quickly. "Want me to give him a taste of ours, King?"

Major Kong frowned judiciously. "We ain't up here to play games, Dietrich. You jest tend to your own business back there."

Dietrich shrugged his shoulders eloquently, removed his attention from the scope, and picked up his cards again.

Beside him Goldberg, who had been dozing over his magazine, suddenly jerked into life as the tone alarm of the combat warning and interference elimination sounded. Of all the highly secret equipment carried in the bomber, it was the most guarded. It received coded messages from Burpelson, but also, if the necessity ever arose, it served as a safeguard against enemy interference in transmitting fake messages designed to deceive and divert the bomber.

Goldberg hastily reached for his code book and flipped through it until he found the appropriate section. While doing this he said, "Got a message from base, King."

King was absently regarding his nails, his mind still fully occupied with his regrettable lack of combat. He said, "What the hell do *they* want?"

Goldberg had now decoded the message. He said, "I have it, King. Wing to hold at Fail-Safe points."

Instantly there was a burst of annoyed reaction from the crew. Lothar Zogg gave it as his opinion that it was probably some kind of exercise. Sweets Kivel threw down his *Confectioner's Journal* and complained loudly that after fourteen hours he was a bit beat. The others agreed they were beat too.

King was seriously annoyed. Like most flyers he had little affection for the staff officers back at base. He said, "Now ain't that jest like them damned armchair commandos back there to keep us up here fer nothin'!"

There was general agreement from the crew. Then an even more annoying factor occurred to King. He turned to Ace Owens. "Boy," he said, "we fool around here too long, we gonna miss our *date*. You know that, don't you?"

Ace Owens nodded glumly and King angrily reached forward and adjusted the autopilot so that *Leper Colony* went into a shallow port bank, ten miles above the icy Barents Sea.

BURPELSON AIR FORCE BASE

An Air Force base by its very nature can seldom be described as beautiful. Yet Burpelson, with pale moonlight casting grotesque shadows of hangars and airplanes onto the concrete of its servicing areas, had a strangely, eerily attractive appearance.

The vast runways were empty, and no pulsing roar of jet engines, which was the normal concomitant of a working day, could be heard. The desert silence was broken only by the giant cicadas and the occasional shrill whine of an electric tool.

Overhead the sky was clear and through the clear desert air the stars shone with an almost luminous brightness. It was a peaceful night.

Sixty feet below the main administration building six officers manned the Command Bridge of the Base Combat Operations Center. Five of them were U.S.A.F. officers; the sixth, and the senior of those present, was from the Royal Air Force. His name was Mandrake—Group Captain Lionel Mandrake D.S.O., D.F.C., R.A.F.

Mandrake's presence in the center was due to the exchange scheme which had long operated between the U.S.A.F. and the R.A.F. It was a scheme regarded with great approval by the authorities and even greater approval by the participants. They were always treated by their hosts as honored guests. They received invitations to all the cocktail parties on the base, and since the saying *le goût d'etranger* is not altogether without foundation, there were other invitations also.

Mandrake was in his second year of duty at Burpelson. He had greatly enjoyed himself there, though he sometimes found it hard to understand the quirkish and peculiar sense of humor which his commanding officer displayed. Mandrake was a man of medium height and build. His uniform was immaculate, with the four broad rings of a group captain on the sleeve and a healthy display of decorations and campaign medals below his pilot's wings. His hair was long by U.S.A.F. standards, but this was understood to be an eccentricity which all R.A.F. officers were prone to. His upper lip sported a bushy and luxuriant mustache. He was chewing absently on the end of a pencil and watching the hands of the big wall clock slowly creep around to the end of his period of duty when the phone near his right hand buzzed.

This was the direct line from General Ripper. Mandrake hastily removed the end of the pencil from his mouth and picked up the phone. He said, "Combat Operations Center, Group Captain Mandrake speaking."

The gruff and unmistakeable tone of General Ripper's voice announced. "This is General Ripper speaking."

"Yes, sir."

"You know it's General Ripper, Group Captain?"

"Why certainly, General," Mandrake said. "Why do you ask, sir?"

"Why do you think I ask, Group Captain?"

Mandrake laughed nervously. "Well, I really don't

know, sir. I mean, we just spoke a few minutes ago, didn't we?"

Ripper's voice had an edge to it now. "You don't think that I'd ask unless it was important, do you, Group Captain?"

"No, sir," Mandrake said nervously, "I'm sure you wouldn't."

"Well, that's better, Group Captain. Let's see if we can stay on the ball."

"Yes, sir.

"Has the wing confirmed holding at their Fail-Safe points?"

"Yes, sir, the confirmations have just come in. All of them."

"All right, Group Captain. Now listen to me very carefully. I'm putting the base on condition Red."

Mandrake started in surprise. He held the phone slightly away from him, recovered his breath, and then said, "Condition Red, sir?"

"That's right," Ripper growled, "condition *Red*. I want it flashed to all sections immediately."

"But what's happened, sir?"

For a few seconds there was silence on the line. To Mandrake it seemed like an eternity. He wondered if perhaps the General had been cut off, but then Ripper spoke again. Ripper said, slowly and as if he had given the matter some considerable thought, "It looks like we're in a global war."

"A global war, sir?"

"Yes, Group Captain. I'm afraid this looks like it's going to be *it*."

"Good Lord!" Mandrake said. "Have they hit anything yet?"

"Group Captain, that's all I've been told. It just came in on the Red phone and my orders call for the base to be sealed tight. And that is precisely what I mean to do."

"But won't that put us a bit, so to speak, out of the picture, sir?"

"You let me worry about that, Group Captain," Ripper said sharply. "I'm commanding officer around here, that's my worry."

"Yes, sir," Mandrake said. His face had all the mournfulness of a disappointed walrus. "Naturally, sir."

Ripper realized immediately from his tone that Mandrake was insulted. He was basically a kindhearted man, and he hastened to make amends. "See here, Group Captain, we don't want to be vulnerable to commie saboteurs, do we?"

Mandrake was slightly reassured. "I see what you mean, sir."

"Then you have it straight, do you? You know the plan?"

Mandrake hedged. "The plan, sir?"

Ripper sighed. Mandrake was not quick, but he was reliable and loyal. Ripper said, "That's right, Group Captain. Operation Oyster."

"Oh, that! Yes, sir," Mandrake said enthusiastically. He thought quickly about Operation Oyster, reviewing the main points of it in his mind.

Ripper said, "Well, are we on the ball?"

Mandrake chuckled. He had a rich, British chuckle. "Oh yes, sir. But I say, I was just thinking of one of the points in the operation order. Something's just occurred to me. How do I know I'm talking to you now?"

"Are you trying to be funny, Mandrake?"

"No, sir," Mandrake said hastily, "not at all."

"Well then," Ripper said slowly and ominously, "just who the hell do you think you're talking to?"

"To you, naturally, sir. But if you take my point, I mean to say, that is, how is one to be sure, sir?"

Ripper paused a moment before replying. He felt it better to do so in the interests of American-Anglo relations. He breathed deeply three times, a practice his mother had taught him to cool his temper. Then he said slowly and carefully, "Group Captain, are you deliberately trying to be insubordinate?"

"Of course not, sir," Mandrake said. There was both hurt and indignation in his voice.

"All right, Group Captain, then let's stay on the ball."

"Yes, sir."

"Okay then," Ripper said briskly, "do you have a pencil in your hand?"

"I'll get one, sir." Mandrake fumbled on the desk for the pencil on which he had previously been chewing and picked it up.

"While you're implementing Operation Oyster, get the Go-code out to the boys."

Mandrake said, "The Go-code, sir?"

"Yeah, yeah, yeah. Go-code, Ultech."

"May I have your confirmation on that, sir?" Mandrake said firmly.

"That's correct, Ultech. That is to be a transmission using the emergency base attack code group."

"Yes, sir. As a transmission using the emergency base attack code group. You will have to give me the code prefix, General."

Ripper said, "What's the matter, Group Captain, don't you have it?"

"Why no, sir. I believe you're the only one on the base who knows it."

General Ripper opened the folder that was lying in front of him on his desk. He said, "You're quite right, Group Captain. It is attack code index Fox-George-Dog, Fox-George-Dog, please repeat."

Mandrake repeated the code.

"Good," Ripper said, "very good. As soon as you've done that, I want you to come on up here to my office."

"But," Mandrake said, "if I do that, there'll be no one in control down here."

"*Are you questioning my orders, Group Captain?*" Ripper snarled.

Mandrake instinctively rose to his feet and assumed a position of attention, holding the telephone rigidly to his ear while Ripper's voice continued with various uncomplimentary epithets.

When it paused, Mandrake said quickly, "Sir, I am not questioning your orders, simply bringing the facts to your attention."

Ripper's fingers drummed on the desk top. He breathed deeply the regulation three times. Then he said, "You're a good officer, Group Captain, and you're perfectly within your rights to bring these facts to my attention, but I am in command here and when I issue orders I expect them carried out. Perhaps we do things a bit differently than you do in the R.A.F."

That, Mandrake thought, was an understatement. But General Ripper was his commanding officer and he replied loyally, "Yes, sir, of course."

"All right then, as soon as you've done that, I want you to get reports on base security. I want the base perimeter defended and I want road blocks set up a half-mile from the base. These commies are plenty smart and we can't rule out the possibility of an attack by saboteurs."

Mandrake, still rigidly at attention, snapped, "Yes, sir, will do."

Ripper heard Mandrake's quick affirmative, then put down his phone. He leaned back in his chair. Maybe in a little while he could relax, maybe even take a small shot of grain alcohol and pure water. But that was for later. There was still lots of work to do. He sighed and reached for another of his telephones.

LEPER COLONY

Inside *Leper Colony*, which was now circling gently in the vicinity of its Fail-Safe point, the crew were engaged in much the same tasks as when they had received the order to hold in that area.

Lieutenant Goldberg's attention was suddenly and unpleasantly disturbed by a clicking from the CWIE. He watched with vague interest while letters and numerals clicked into place on the dials, reached for his code book, and began decoding. When he had finished, he frowned in puzzlement, tapped the defense-systems officer, Lieutenant Dietrich, lightly on the shoulder to draw his attention, and showed him the message pad.

"Some screwy joker," Dietrich said briefly and returned to the new card trick he was trying to perfect.

Goldberg frowned again, thought for a moment, then switched on his intercom. He said, "Hey, King, get a load of this off the CWIE. Just come through. It says, 'Attack using Ultech.'"

King considered the matter. He repeated the message musingly. "Now what the hell they talkin' about?"

"Attack using Ultech," Goldberg repeated. "That's exactly what it says."

Captain Ace Owens lowered his magazine. He looked across at King. "Is he kidding?"

King said firmly, "Well, check your code again, that just can't be right."

"I *have* checked it again," Goldberg said.

King gestured to Ace, indicating that he was in executive command of the flight deck. He stood up slowly, then said, "Goldy, you must have made a mistake, Goldy."

"I'm telling you, goddammit," Goldberg said irately, "that's how it decodes. You don't believe me, you come and see for yourself."

The whole crew had heard this interchange. From the lower deck Lothar Zogg and Sweets Kivel emerged and crowded with King around Goldberg and Dietrich. Ace Owens, leaving the plane to cruise on autopilot, went back to join the group.

Goldberg held out the code book to King. "Here," he said, "you want to check it yourself?"

King looked at the book briefly, then he said, "All right, git a confirmation on that, Goldberg. Don't you mention the message, you hear, jest ask fer confirmation."

Goldberg manipulated various switches on the machine. The whole crew watched as first the letters and numerals disappeared, then reappeared exactly as before. There were a few moments of absolute silence while they thought about the unthinkable.

King scratched his head. He said, "You know, I'm beginnin' to work to certain conclusions."

In the silence of the next few moments, while they thought about it, the expressions of the crew became grim. Slowly they all turned toward King, waiting for him to say the definitive word.

When King spoke, it was with quiet dignity. "Well, boys, I reckon this is it."

"What?" Ace Owens said.

"*Com*-bat."

"But we're carrying hydrogen bombs," Lothar Zogg muttered.

King nodded gravely in assent. "That's right, *nuclear com*-bat! Toe-to-toe with the Russkies."

Lothar Zogg said thoughtfully and with a note of hope in his voice, "Maybe it's just some kind of screwball exercise, just to see if we're on our toes. You know the kind of thing they're always dreaming up to check on us."

King made a cutting motion with his right hand, dismissing the idea. "Shoot," he said, "they ain't sendin' us in there with this load on no exercise, that's for damn sure."

"Yeah, but it could be sort of a loyalty test. You know, give the Go-code and then the Recall, just to find out who would actually go."

"Now listen to me, Lothar," King said, "that's the Go-code! It's never been given to anyone before and it would never be given as a test."

Having delivered himself of this ultimate statement, King turned back to the pilot's compartment alone. The others continued to discuss the matter, at first in hushed, somber tones.

"It's going to be rough on the folks back home," Sweets Kivel said.

"Yeah," Dietrich agreed, "really rough."

Ace Owens said, "But how could it have started? It wasn't supposed to happen."

Sweets agreed with him. "That's what I can't figure. Just how it could have started."

Meanwhile, alone in the pilot's compartment, King sat in his seat gazing at his ancestral portraits. He fixed on the portrait of Bull Daddy Dawson. There was affection in his gaze and pride too. He said softly as he leaned forward and touched the portrait lightly, "Well, ole Bull Daddy, mebbe you won't be top gun much longer." He became aware that the others were still yakking in a group around Goldberg.

Goldberg was becoming more and more excited. "Those bastards must have hit us!" he said.

"That's right," Dietrich said loudly. "*We* wouldn't have started it."

King turned in his seat. Goldberg and Dietrich became suddenly aware of his jaundiced appraisal.

King said calmly but coldly, "Okay, so we've been hit. Awright, so where does that leave us? I tell you where it leaves us. We got to hit back! *R*eprisal! That's the way it is, they hit us, we got to reprise. Ain't that right?"

Dietrich exchanged glances with Goldberg. Both of them nodded their heads in assent. King was right, they both realized that.

Goldberg climbed out of his seat and made his way forward. His expression was sheepish. He stuck his hand out to Major Kong.

Having made his point, King once more became his usual affable self. He grasped Goldberg's hand and shook it energetically.

King said, "Fergit it, Goldy. It could happen to the best of us. Now let's get squared away, fellas, we got some flyin' to do." He watched with paternal affection as the crew got back to their positions and prepared to commence their combat drills.

Dietrich opened a small safe and from among a dozen others selected a thick sealed envelope clearly marked "Ultech." He held it up so King could see the marking. King looked at it closely and satisfied himself it was the correct envelope.

"Okay," he said, "open her up." He watched with grave approval while Dietrich broke open the seal and extracted from the envelope six individual folders, one for each of the crew.

Sweets Kivel, the navigator, said through the inter-com, "First course is one-seven-five. Let you have a more accurate figure when I've plotted it. Shouldn't take more than a minute."

King leaned forward and adjusted his gyro. The great bomber banked, and turned automatically to the new heading.

As it turned, King read from his folder, which was the master copy. "Okay. Here's the check list. Complete radio silence. The CWIE is to operate as of now. The emergency base-code index for recall is to be set on the dials of the CWIE. Okay, Goldy, you get that?"

"Roger. I'm setting it up."

As Goldberg set the CWIE, Sweets came up with the heading. "One-seven-eight, King."

"Roger. One-seven-eight." King leaned forward to adjust his gyro and again the plane banked to starboard toward the new heading.

King again read from his folder. "Primary target the ICBM complex at Laputa. First weapon fused for air burst. Your second weapon will be used if first malfunc-tions. Otherwise proceed to secondary target. Borchav, that missile base. Fused air burst. Any questions?"

The crew had no questions.

King went on. "Okay now, in about ten minutes we start losing altitude to keep under their radar. We'll cross in over the coast about fifteen thousand, then drop low level to the primary. Okay, boys, now how about some hot Java?"

WASHINGTON

The Fabulous Hotel occupied an entire city block. Architecturally it was a monstrosity, but throughout its eighteen floors it offered luxury of almost Oriental opulence to those who could afford to stay there. These fortunate people were for the most part top government officers and military chiefs, successful lobbyists and members of Congress.

On the seventeenth floor, in suite 1704, the Chief of the Joint Chiefs of Staff was in residence. His name was General Turgidson, known to his many associates as "Buck." He was presently enjoying a cooling and relaxing shower while his secretary, who was known to the crew of *Leper Colony* as Miss Foreign Affairs, was lying on her stomach on a bed.

Miss Foreign Affairs, a tall shapely brunette, was dressed in a spotted bikini which did more to emphasize than conceal her figure. Over the sound of General Buck Turgidson singing under the shower a telephone rang insistently. Miss Foreign Affairs raised her head, got up on her knees, and looked at the phone. She called out, "Buck, should I get it?"

Turgidson's voice came from inside the bathroom. He said, "Yeah, you'll have to."

Miss Foreign Affairs switched off the sun lamp under which she had been basking, got off the bed, and leaned forward to pick up the receiver.

"Hello... Oh yes, General Turgidson is here, but I'm afraid he can't come to the phone right now... Oh, this is his secretary Miss Wood. Freddie, how are you?... Just fine, thank you... Oh, we were just catching up on some of the General's paper work... Well, look, Freddie, he's all tied up right at the moment I'm afraid. He can't pos-

sibly come to the phone... Oh, I see, just a second...
General Turgidson, Colonel Puntrich is calling."

Turgidson shouted from the bathroom, "Tell him to
call back."

The girl said quickly into the telephone, "Freddie, the
General says could you call back in a minute or two...
oh I see. It can't wait."

Again Turgidson's voice was heard. "Ah, for Pete's
sake. Well, find out what he wants."

"Freddie, the thing is the General is in the powder
room right now. Could you tell me what it's about?...
Buck, apparently they monitored a transmission about
eight minutes ago from Burpelson Air Force Base. It was
directed to the bomb wing on airborne patrol. It decoded as Ultech—Attack."

The sound of water died away. Turgidson was
annoyed. He said, "Er...um...tell him to call what's-his-
name...the base commander, Ripper. Do I have to think
of everything around this place?"

Miss Wood—or Miss Foreign Affairs—said, "Freddie,
are you there? Well listen, the General suggests you call
General Ripper...oh I see... You mean all communications are dead?"

Turgidson said loudly, "Tell him to check on that personally."

Miss Wood said quickly, "The General suggests you
try him again yourself...oh I see." She covered the
mouthpiece of the telephone with her hand and spoke
toward the bathroom. "He says he's tried several times
but just can't get General Ripper to answer."

General Buck Turgidson padded out of the bathroom
wearing a dazzling robe. He took the receiver from his
secretary, who knelt on the pillow of the bed and got a
cigarette from her handbag.

Turgidson said, "Fred, Buck here. What's it look like.

Ah...ah yeah...is it really Ultech? Hah...well...well, what's cooking on the threat board?... Nothing!" He moved his head to the right to allow his secretary to put a cigarette in his mouth. "Nothing at all... I don't like the look of this, Fred...ah yeah...tell you what you'd better do, old buddy. You give Elmo and Charlie a blast, bump everything up to condition Red and stand by the blower. I'll get back to you." He replaced the receiver.

Miss Wood looked at him. Her big, liquid eyes were devoted. She said, "What's up, honey?"

Turgidson said, "Nothing. Where's my shorts?"

"On the floor. Where are you going?"

Turgidson moved round to the far side of the other bed. He said, "No place special. I just thought I'd mosey over to the War Room, see what's going on there." He bent and picked up his underwear from the floor.

"But it's three o'clock in the morning!"

Turgidson quickly slipped on his shorts and then shucked off his robe. He said, "Well, the Air Force never sleeps."

Miss Wood lay back on the bed. She said, "Buck, honey. I'm not sleepy either." There was a quality in her voice that made Turgidson turn quickly to look at her.

Turgidson said, "Ah, I know how it is, baby." He crawled across the second bed where she was lying. He said fondly, "Tell you what you do. Look, you start your count down right now and old Buckie will be back here before you can say re-entry."

She looked at him fondly and reached out a hand to stroke his short bristling hair. Then she brought up her other arm around his neck and clasped him tightly to her.

BURPELSON AIR FORCE BASE

The calm and peaceful atmosphere which had previously existed that night at Burpelson had been violently shattered by General Ripper's orders to seal tight the base.

Squads of armed men moved purposefully in all directions, and in many places machine-gun teams were digging in their weapons to command the approaches to the base. Grenades had been issued to those thought competent to handle them, that is, to those who would be less dangerous to their own men than the enemy. There were not many of these, for Burpelson was primarily an air base, and a good mechanic is not necessarily a good combat soldier. However, over a thousand men were now deployed in defense of the base, and General Ripper watched their activities from his huge armored window with approval and satisfaction.

He turned away from the window and walked over to his desk, picked up a hand microphone, and switched on the public-address system. He began to speak. This of course was normal procedure. Whenever he had something of importance to say, the commanding general always addressed his troops.

All over the base his voice echoed metallically from the big speakers. Men paused in their activities to listen to him, for Ripper was admired and respected by most of the men he commanded.

"...why I am speaking to you at this moment. Many of you may never have seen a nuclear device exploded and because of this may have some exaggerated concern about casualties.

"Let me frankly assure you, as your commanding officer, there is very little difference between an ordinary bullet and an H-bomb, except possibly a matter of degree, maybe a lot smaller degree than all these *experts* say. But there is one thing I have learned—if your number's up there is nothing you can do about it, and one way or another it amounts to the same thing."

An airman digging in a machine gun on the main approach road to the base nudged his buddy in the ribs. He said, "Well, I never thought of it that way before. The old man sure makes it clear. Whatever it is, you're just as dead."

"That's right," the other airman replied, "we're just as dead."

Ripper's voice went on. "…but there are other types of attack—they are detailed on the operation order—which could be fatal to us here at Burpelson."

Ripper then detailed the orders required by Operation Oyster. These included: (a) To defend the Constitution of the United States whatever may be the outcome of this defense. (b) To obey without question the orders of the commanding officer and of him alone. (c) To suspect and to fire upon saboteurs, however friendly they may appear to be. (d) To hold our belief in God and rely on the purity of our bodily essences.

Ripper paused, cleared his throat, and reached for a glass of the rain water he had poured before he began to speak to his men. Then he continued: "Now I know you men are familiar with the details of this order and I don't think there's one of you here will let me down, but I thought it was best to repeat the prime details to you, in all our interests."

Again he paused, but this time to master the overwhelming emotion, which he was sure would otherwise be reflected in his voice and might affect the men. He did not want them misty-eyed when they might need clear vision to engage the enemy. He succeeded in controlling his emotion and then continued in his normal tone.

"In conclusion, men, I'd like to say that in the two years that I have been privileged to be your commanding officer, I have always expected the best from you and you have never given me anything less than that. Good luck to you all."

He sank back in his chair and lit a cigar. He felt tired now, but he also felt an enormous inner satisfaction. It was done. The base was sealed tight. Operation Oyster had been implemented. He knew his boys would never let him down.

The door of his office opened and Group Captain Mandrake entered.

LEPER COLONY

In the narrow, confined space between the pilot's compartment and the position where the defense-systems officer and radar/radio officer sat, the five members of the crew were crowded together facing King. It was a solemn moment.

Beside him, piled on his seat, which he had vacated while the plane cruised on autopilot, were six plastic packages looking like boys' Christmas surprise parcels.

King picked up one of the packages and held it up so everyone could see it. He addressed the crew, who maintained a respectful silence.

He said, "Okay, boys, I have to hand out these survival kits before we go over enemy territory. In them you will find"—he began to read on the reverse side of the package— "one .45 automatic; two boxes ammunition; four days' concentrated emergency rations; one fishing line and hooks; six plastic worms for use with fishing line; one pocketknife; one compass; one drug issue containing antibiotic pills, morphine pills, vitamin pills, pep pills, sleeping pills, tranquilizer pills; one miniature combination Russian phrase book and Bible; one hundred dollars in gold; four 21-jewel Swiss watches; one hundred dollars in rubles; five gold-plated fountain pens; ten packs chewing gum; one issue prophylactics; three lipsticks; three pairs nylon stockings."

The check list finished, King then handed out one of the packages to each of the crew, who stepped forward in turn to receive it. His own package he stowed away at the side of his seat.

And *Leper Colony* continued smoothly and on schedule toward the enemy coast.

THE PENTAGON

It is said that the state of world tension can be accurately assessed by estimating the number of lights which burn through the night at the Pentagon. Normally there are few. They burn in the rooms of the duty officers, the cipher staffs, and other officials whose offices need to be manned through all the hours of the day and all the days of every year. On this night many more lights than usual burned in the vast building.

Inside the building there were many elevators. One of

these had been seen by very few people. It was now descending to a level hundreds of feet below the ground floor. The doors of the elevator slid open and a huddle of men emerged, rapidly fanning out into a protective cordon, which moved briskly down the bare corridor that confronted the elevator doors.

The secret-service men who comprised this escort, ten in number, ran at a good clip to keep up with the swiftly moving object they were protecting. The object was a small electric car in which sat Merkin Muffley, President of the United States.

As the car moved along, with its heavily breathing escort, past immaculate and alert carbine-equipped guards who lined the walls of the corridor at intervals of twenty-five feet, President Muffley was utilizing a battery-powered electric shaver. The party pressed on through the labyrinthine corridor, then came to a halt facing a heavy metal door, above which was inscribed the sign: CATEGORY ONE—MAXIMUM SECURITY AREA. The President, after running an exploratory hand round his face, slipped the shaver back into its slot and stepped out of the car.

The metal door was guarded by a captain and two sergeants, armed respectively with a .45 automatic and machine carbines. The three men snapped smartly to attention as the President, now flanked by his secret-service men, walked toward them.

The President stopped in front of the captain. He said absently, "Good morning, Captain," at the same time motioning with his hand for the door to be opened.

The captain, rigidly at attention, his face a model of military impassiveness, permitted his lips to move enough to say, "Good morning, sir. Your pass, please."

President Muffley frowned and fumbled hurriedly through his pockets. Then he said, "Well now, I'm sorry, Captain. I'm afraid I left my wallet in my bedroom."

He stepped forward but the captain blocked his way, at the same time saying, "I'm sorry, sir. This is a maximum security area. Security Regulations, one thirty-four-B—Section seven—Sub-Section D—item six, require..."

"We know all that," the chief of the secret-service men said. Then he lowered his voice to denote respect.

"This is the *President*, Captain." The captain remained immobile and impassive. The President said, "You do recognize me, I take it, Captain?"

"Yes, sir. I believe I do, sir, but Security Regulations, one thirty-four-B—Section seven—Sub-Section D—item six, state definitely that White House I.D. pass will be surrendered by all personnel entering the War Room. There may be no exception to this regulation, sir."

President Muffley shuffled his feet embarrassedly. He said, "Captain, this is a very awkward and unfortunate situation. The National Security Council is already assembled and waiting for me on a matter of the gravest urgency. Even minutes may count. You have my personal assurance that the rules may be overlooked on this occasion."

"I'm sorry, sir, I cannot allow you to enter. Security Regulations, one thirty-four-B—Section seven—Sub Section D—item six..."

As he spoke the President gave an imperceptible sign to the chief of the secret-service men. The entire escort rushed the captain and his two sergeants and overwhelmed them in a welter of heaving bodies. The chief stepped forward and opened the door for the President to enter, then followed him into the room, accompanied by two secret-service men who had not been involved in the fracas.

The room was large and rectangular. It was completely bare of furniture except for a single chair placed at its center. The President walked rapidly to the chair and settled himself into it comfortably. Then he produced a handkerchief with which he wiped his streaming eyes. He was suffering from a severe cold and a persistent headache.

The two secret-service men waited deferentially for the President to finish using his handkerchief. Then, when he had tucked it away in his pocket, they stepped forward and strapped him securely into the chair. The chief had meanwhile moved across to the wall which was decorated only by one large hand switch. He was standing beside the switch, poised and ready to operate it at the President's signal.

The President looked at him and said, "Hold it a moment, Charlie. Get this thing straightened out, will you? Send somebody back for the pass."

"Yes sir," the chief said. "All set, sir?"

The President nodded his grave assent. The chief threw the switch and the chair rose rapidly and smoothly on a hydraulic shaft straight toward the ceiling. Unfortunately, due to some mechanical malfunction it did not rise completely and came to a stop some feet below the ceiling.

The President blew his nose and gestured irritably to the chief, who threw the switch rapidly several times while the President fumed with impatience.

Finally it worked and the chair rose again, up and out of sight through the trap door in the ceiling.

THE WAR ROOM

The room was vast, cavernous, with sloping concrete walls that came together at the apex of the tri-
angle they formed with the black, shining floor.

One of these walls was decorated by a series of displays which gave vital information on all aspects of the
national defense to those who were privileged to see it.
The displays were presented in a series of illuminated
charts, and at a glance it was possible to view the situation as it changed.

On the extreme left was a display showing a polar
projection of the United States and Russia. This was
linked to the Ballistic Missile Early Warning System, two
bases in the U.S. and one in the U.K. It would give visual indication of any rocket trajectories detected by them.

Next was a display showing the number of SAC
bombers available, and their readiness state. It also
showed the number of U.S. missiles and how long it
would take to make them ready to go.

On the right of this indicator there was a projection
of the United States, extending north as far as the Arctic.
On this could be seen any build-up of Russian bomber
forces in the north, and also the submarines which were
within missile range of the American coast.

Next came the biggest display—a projection of
Russia and its surrounding territory and sea. Here
would be shown the precomputed tracks of SAC
bombers as they headed toward their assigned targets.
The targets could also be shown. Primary targets were
represented by triangles, and secondary targets by
squares. These targets were mostly missile and bomber
bases, with a few radar positions and defensive missile
complexes. Some were near big centers of population,

some were not. But it was impossible to tell from the display. Centers of population were not shown.

There were also other displays showing global weather conditions, fallout possibilities, and the disposition of NATO and Russian forces, land, sea, and air, in Europe and the Mediterranean.

The series of displays was known affectionately to those who conducted global strategy as the "Big Board."

These men were now seated round a huge circular table covered with green cloth and with recessed telephones built into it. Above them a suspended ring of lights shone down on each man's position. The air was thick with cigarette smoke.

They waited expectantly for the sound of the trap door and the appearance of the President's balding head and thick spectacles.

As the President's chair rose into the one vacant position at the table, twenty-two men who were already seated round it rose to their feet. One did not, because he was seated in a wheelchair, which he could not leave without assistance. However, he jerked his head as a mark of respect. His name was Doctor Strangelove. President Muffley blew his nose vigorously then said, "Good morning, gentlemen. Please sit down. Is everyone here?"

Staines, one of the presidential aides, said, "Mister President, the Secretary of State is in Vietnam, the Secretary of Defense is in Laos, and the Vice President is in Mexico City. We can establish contact with them at any time if it is necessary."

"Fine, fine," the President said absently, then looked toward General Buck Turgidson, the Air Force Chief of the Joint Chiefs of Staff. "Now, Buck, what the hell's going on here?"

General Turgidson rose smartly to his feet. As usual,

there was a slight smile on his face. Those who knew him well were not deceived by it. He was dressed now in full uniform and on his shoulders the four stars of his rank gleamed under the overhead light. He said, "Well now, Mister President, there appears to be a bit of a problem."

The President said, "Obviously. I don't expect to be got out of my bed at this hour unless there *is* a problem. Just what is the nature of this problem?"

Turgidson said, "Mister President, it appears that over thirty bombers of one of our airborne alert wings have been ordered to attack their targets inside Russia. The planes are fully loaded with nuclear weapons with an average load of forty megatons each. The central display of Russia will indicate the planes' positions—the triangles are their primary targets, the squares are their secondary targets. The aircraft will begin penetrating Russian radar cover inside twenty-five minutes from now."

Doctor Strangelove looked keenly at the President as he absorbed General Turgidson's information. The President seemed worried, Strangelove thought, while Turgidson seemed confident and happy. Strangelove was not unhappy himself. Though he was known personally to few people in this room, he had long exerted an influence on United States defense policy. He was a recluse and perhaps had been made so by the effects of the British bombing of Peenemünde, where he was working on the German V-2 rocket. His black-gloved right hand was a memento of this. He was not sure whether he disliked the British more than the Russians. He gazed out through myopic eyes, which were assisted by frameless bifocals, at the duel between the President and General Turgidson, whom he had never met.

Turgidson continued. "Yes, sir, seems like General

Ripper of Burpelson Air Force Base—one of our finest bases, sir—decided to go for the Russians with his planes."

President Muffley passed a hand across his forehead. "I find this very difficult to understand, General," he said. "I am the only one who has authority to order the use of nuclear weapons."

Turgidson's smile widened slightly, as it always did when he was in a tight situation. He said gravely, "That's right, sir. You are the only person so authorized. I hate to judge before all the facts are in, but it's beginning to look like General Ripper kind of exceeded his authority."

"But that's *impossible*," the President snapped.

"Perhaps you're forgetting the provisions of Ultech, sir?"

President Muffley shook his head in puzzlement. "Ultech?"

Turgidson said quickly, "That's right, sir. Ultech. It is what the code name implies—that the ultimate lowest echelon will be able to take effective action. Surely you must recall—Ultech is an emergency war plan in which a lower echelon commander can order nuclear retaliation after a sneak attack if the normal chain of command has been disrupted. You approved it, sir. Surely you must remember, sir, when Senator Duff made that big hassle about our deterrent lacking credibility. The idea was for Ultech to be a sort of retaliatory safeguard."

"What do you mean, a safeguard?"

"Well, sir, I admit the human element seems to have failed us here, but the idea was to discourage the Russkies from any hope that they could knock out Washington and yourself as part of a sneak attack and escape retaliation because of lack of proper command and control."

"All right," President Muffley said, "all right. Has

there been any indication whatsoever of hostile Russian intentions in the last twenty-four hours?"

"No, sir, there has not. The more I think about it this really is beginning to look like a very unfortunate misuse of Ultech."

The President glanced at the central display, where the bomber tracks were seen steadily converging on Russia. Then he looked down at a pad in front of him and drew a few speculative lines on it while he thought. He looked at Turgidson again. "Well now," he said, "all right. But I assume the planes will return automatically as soon as they reach their Fail-Safe points."

Turgidson had remained standing while the President thought. He said, "No, sir, I'm afraid not. The planes were holding at their Fail-Safe point when the Go-code was issued. Once they fly beyond Fail-Safe they do not require a second order to proceed. They will continue until they reach their targets."

"Well, why haven't you radioed the planes countermanding the Go-code?"

"I'm afraid we're unable to communicate with any of the aircraft."

"But this is absurd," the President said sharply.

Turgidson smiled his preliminary smile. "As you may recall, Mister President, one of the provisions of Ultech is that once the Go-code is received the normal Single Side Band radios in the aircraft are switched into a specially coded device, which I believe is designated CWIE. To prevent the enemy from issuing fake or confusing orders the CWIE is designed not to receive at all unless the message is preceded by the correct code group prefix."

President Muffley said, "Well, but surely this is part of the SAC master code?"

"No, sir, it is not. Since this is an emergency war plan and has to be activated at a lower echelon, the lower

echelon commander designates the code, and in this case
it is known only to General Ripper, since he changed it
just before take-off and gave it personally to the crews
at their pre-flight briefing."

President Muffley said slowly, "Then do you mean to
say you will be unable to recall the aircraft?"

"I'm afraid that's about the size of it, sir. We are plow-
ing through every possible combination of the code, but
there are many thousand combinations and it will take
us several days to transmit them all."

"How soon did you say the planes would penetrate
Russian radar cover?"

"About eighteen minutes from now, sir."

"Are you in contact with General Ripper?" The
President's voice was brisk and authoritative now.

"No, sir. General Ripper has sealed off his base and cut
off all communications. We are unable to get through to
him."

"Then where the hell," the President demanded, "did
you get all this information?"

"Sir, General Ripper called Strategic Air Command
Headquarters shortly after he issued the Go-code. I have
a portion of the transcript of the conversation here, if
you'd like me to read it."

The President nodded his head in assent.

"The duty officer asked General Ripper to confirm
the fact that he had issued the Go-code and he said, 'Yes,
gentlemen, they are on their way in and no one can
bring them back. For the sake of our country and our
way of life I suggest you get the rest of SAC in after
them, otherwise we will be totally destroyed by Red
retaliation. So let's get going, there's no other choice.
God willing, we shall prevail in peace and freedom from
fear and in true health through the purity and essence of
our natural fluids.' Then he hung up."

President Muffley said, "Did you say something about *fluids?*"

Turgidson looked down at his typescript again, and found the passage. "Yes sir, here it is. 'We shall prevail in peace and freedom from fear and in true health through the purity and essence of our natural fluids.' We are still trying to figure out the meaning of that last phrase, sir."

"There's nothing to figure out, General Turgidson. The man's obviously a psychotic."

"Well, Mister President, I'd like to hold off judgment on a thing like that until all the facts are in."

The President said slowly, "General Turgidson, when you instituted the reliability tests, you assured me that from then on there was no possibility of such a thing ever occurring."

"I don't think it is fair to condemn a whole program for a single slip-up, sir."

President Muffley made a dismissing motion with his hand. "Never mind, we're wasting precious time. I want to speak personally to General Ripper on the telephone."

"I'm afraid that will be impossible, sir."

President Muffley drummed his fingers on the table. He made an obvious effort to control himself, but then burst out, "General, I am beginning to have less and less interest in your estimates of what is possible or impossible."

Around the table everyone was silent. They glanced covertly at the crimson-faced but still sickly smiling General, and the President's expression of tightly controlled fury.

After ten seconds, which seemed to stretch into hours, Turgidson said, "Mister President, if I may speak for General Faceman, Admiral Randolph, our aides, our staff, we are all professionals, sir. We've spent our lives at this and we know our jobs. All the contingencies are being considered and you may rest assured that the departments concerned are on top of this thing. Now, we can all understand what kind of strain you must be under, just having been rousted out of a sickbed, and if I may suggest, sir, we are all on the same side. We are all trying to accomplish the same thing, and perhaps it might be the best way if you just let us handle this."

When the President replied, his voice, though still tightly controlled, had in it a quality of quiet fury. "General Turgidson, I want one thing understood and understood clearly—I am running this! I am running this right to the end! It is my responsibility and my right, and anyone who feels his professional talents are not receiving sufficient recognition may hand in his resignation, which will be instantly accepted!"

"Well now," Turgidson said, "Mister President, we're here to help you, sir, and there was certainly no offense meant by that remark."

"All right," President Muffley said, "I'll accept that. General Faceman, are there any army units near Burpelson?"

"One moment, sir." General Faceman turned to a colonel sitting next to him, and they conferred hastily in hushed whispers. Then Faceman, a stocky gray-haired man in his middle forties, said, "Yes, sir. I believe there's an airborne division positioned about seven miles away at Alvarado."

"Very well," the President said. In spite of his cold, his voice was clear and incisive. "General Faceman, I want you to get on the phone yourself and speak to the officer in charge. Tell him to get himself and his men moving immediately. If they don't have enough vehicles, commandeer cars off the highway, but tell him he must be there within fifteen minutes from the time he hangs up the phone. If he can't get them all there, get as many as he can. I want them to enter the base, locate General Ripper, and immediately put him into telephone contact with me."

Staines, the presidential aide, asked a question. "Mister President, what is your feeling about civil defense?"

"Well now," President Muffley said, "civil defense..." He paused and frowned while he considered the matter. He used his inhaler while he thought.

"Shall we let the situation mature a bit, sir?" Staines suggested.

"Why yes," the President said, "yes, I think that's the best policy for the moment." He used his inhaler again as he turned to look at the electronic displays.

Doctor Strangelove looked at the displays also. He noted that the lines indicating bomber tracks were encroaching steadily on Russia. He was not displeased.

LEPER COLONY

Leper Colony was still at high altitude, moving smoothly over high cloud and frozen terrain. But the attack profile called now for a descent to evade Russian radar. There is a definite and predictable pattern in the way radar operates. Radar beams travel in a straight line. But the earth is curved, and therefore by making a low approach it is possible to evade the detecting beams.

Lieutenant Sweets Kivel, the navigator, finished his calculations and glanced at his clock. He waited while the second hand came to the exact place he had planned for, then said, "Make rate of descent fifteen hundred per minute. That should slide us in nicely under their radar cover."

King adjusted the trim and throttled back slowly to maintain the correct speed. *Leper Colony* began to descend steadily at fifteen hundred feet per minute and speed Mach 0.9.

King said, "Descent steady at fifteen hun'erd. Speed steady at Mach zero-nine."

Sweets Kivel glanced at his ground-position indicator, on which certain of the pilot's instruments were duplicated. "Roger. Maintain."

King said, "Okay, ready for checks."

Both the defense-systems officer, Lieutenant Dietrich, and the navigator acknowledged. The navigator spoke first. "Main search radar all green. Set for maximum range, maximum sweep."

King acknowledged.

Lieutenant Dietrich made a final small adjustment to his apparatus. Then satisfied, he said, "Both electronic detectors set to swing from stud A through H."

On the bulky electronic detector a small rotor arm moved rapidly through the sequence of stud setting, each representing a preselected frequency band, then flicked back to start the sequence again.

But Dietrich had not yet finished his checks of the complex equipment. He now glanced at another of his sets and said, "Main interference linked to electronic detector. Fighter interference on readiness state. Target-detection radar is green. Target-illuminating radar is green."

"Check."

"Missile and flight-path computer showing four greens."

"Check."

King's voice was happy as he spoke to Lothar Zogg, the bombardier, whose checks were next on the list. All the equipment was in good shape, so far, and he felt an inner certainty everything was going to be green. He looked fondly at the ancestral triptych as he said, "Lothar, how about it?"

Lothar Zogg replied quickly as he slid a transparency off his radarscope, "Target-approach radar tuning is right. All approach transparencies are checked, one through twenty-five."

"Check target approach."

Lothar went on. "Bomb-door circuit is green, bomb-release circuit is green, bomb-fusing circuit is green." King relaxed in his seat. They were flying. Everything was green. There was nothing would stop them now.

Lothar Zogg asked, "When do you want to arm the bomb for the primary, King?"

"Soon as I've checked out the approach."

After King had spoken, Sweets said, "In thirty seconds the count-down clock should read eighty-three minutes. Eighty-three."

"Roger." King reached forward and set the clock to 83.

BURPELSON AIR FORCE BASE

Group Captain Mandrake walked across General Ripper's office and stopped in front of Ripper's desk.

General Ripper lit a cigar. Then he said thoughtfully,

"Group Captain, you think this officer exchange plan between the U.S.A.F. and the R.A.F. is a good one? I mean, you like it with us?"

"Well of course, sir," Mandrake said. "Naturally."

"Then in that case," Ripper said, "would you please realize you do not have any special prerogative to question orders from your commanding officer?"

And with that, Ripper got up from his seat and said, "Pardon me for a moment, Group Captain," walked across the room, his massive body shaking the floor as he walked, and disappeared into the bathroom that was attached to his office.

Mandrake was suddenly startled by the sound of the Red telephone. He picked up the phone and said, "This is Burpelson." He listened to the message from the other end and said, "Why no, I didn't know that! I mean to say, there isn't any threat? He's done it without orders? No, I don't know any more. He's in the bathroom at the moment—I'll contact him as soon as he comes out... Well dammit, it is rather awkward to disturb one's commanding officer when he's in the bathroom, isn't it?... Well I mean, what's he going to say about one in his annual report?"

Mandrake listened to the blistering reply, winced, and hung up the telephone. He was more than ever sure that these Americans were coarse and vulgar people. But that did not affect the seriousness of the message he had received from the SAC operations controller.

General Ripper came back from the bathroom. Mandrake said slowly, "Sir, with respect, I have an unpleasant duty to do. I have to ask you why you have sent the wing to attack Russia?"

"Because I thought it proper, Group Captain." Ripper's voice was soft. "Why else do you think I'd do it?"

Mandrake started forward impulsively, then paused as

he saw that on the other side of the desk Ripper had produced a .45 automatic, which was pointing at him. From a distance of four or five feet the muzzle of a four-five is unpleasantly wide. Mandrake retreated a pace, then another.

Ripper said pleasantly, "Now please, don't try to leave the room, Group Captain." Mandrake swallowed.

He was eight feet from Ripper now, but the muzzle of the four-five still looked unpleasantly large. He said stiffly, "Are you threatening a brother officer with a gun, sir?"

Ripper laid the gun down on the surface of his desk. "Now look," he said soothingly, "just cool off, Group Captain Mandrake, and pour me a grain alcohol and rain water. Help yourself to whatever you like."

Mandrake crossed the room to the drink cabinet and began to pour out the drinks.

Ripper watched the process with approval. While Mandrake poured he said, "Relax, Group Captain. There's nothing anyone can do about it now. I'm the only man who knows the code."

Mandrake uncorked a bottle of the General's rain water. "How much rain water, sir?"

"About half and half."

Mandrake poured the appropriate amount of rain water into the glasses, then carried them across to the General's desk. He passed one of the glasses to the General, who smiled benevolently and accepted the drink with his left hand, while keeping his right hand over the butt of the automatic that lay on the desk. He said, "And now let's drink a toast, Group Captain."

Years of training had their effect. Mandrake snapped to attention and waited respectfully for the General's toast.

Ripper said, holding up his glass, "To peace on earth and to the purity and essence of our natural fluids." They touched glasses and both of them drank.

Mandrake finished his drink in one gulp. After the realization had come to him that the General had done this thing, there was an inevitable period of shock. His eyes were marbled, and his whole nervous system was reacting violently against the incredibility of the act. Yet, as he looked at Ripper's relaxed, confident face, he knew that incredible or not, it had been done and this man had done it. Was he right? Was it the thing to do?

Group Captain Mandrake simply did not know. On the one hand he liked and admired Ripper, who had not been just a C.O. but a friend to him all the time he had been at Burpelson. On the other, his mind rejected with horror the inevitable consequences of Ripper's action.

His thoughts, chaotic at first, slowly took coherent form. He said, "But look here, General Ripper, with respect, sir, surely you must know the wing can't suppress Russian retaliation on its own. The Reds will hit back with everything they've got, and we know, you and I, that's plenty."

Ripper permitted himself the luxury of a small smile. He was fond of Mandrake, and had enjoyed having him as executive officer. But Mandrake could not appreciate the delightful ripeness of his plan without explanation. General Ripper prepared to give it to him, at the same time savoring in his mind the beautiful artistic balance of the scheme he had devised.

"Now you give it some thought, Group Captain. We will be hit hard only if we don't strike in full strength and at once." He paused, then continued. "And that's exactly what we shall do."

"I don't see how you can possibly know that, sir."

General Ripper examined the glowing end of his cigar with satisfaction. "Group Captain Mandrake," he said, "at this very moment while we sit here and chat so enjoyably, I can assure you a decision is being made by the President and the Joint Chiefs in the War Room at the Pentagon. When they realize there is no possibility of recalling the wing, there will be only one course of action open to them. Total commitment!"

As he spoke, Ripper emphasized his words by beating the side of his fist on the desk. Mandrake watched him, as hypnotically fascinated as a rabbit by a snake. He wondered if the General was right, if even at this moment a major strike against Russia was under way. He thought it probably was. Ripper seemed completely confident what action the President would take.

Mandrake said hesitantly, "Well, I suppose you may be right, General."

"You're damned right I'm right," Ripper said furiously. His eyes narrowed and he looked at Mandrake with a strange expression. "Are you a communist, Group Captain?"

"Oh, good lord no, sir," Mandrake said indignantly. "I'm an officer of the Royal Air Force."

Ripper nodded his head wisely. "Just what I meant. The R.A.F. is full of commies, you know that, Group Captain?"

Mandrake was too shaken to make any reply.

Ripper went on. "You know, Group Captain, I visited a lot of R.A.F. bases during the war. You know what I saw written on the walls at a lot of them?"

Mandrake shook his head dumbly.

" 'Joe for King,' Group Captain, that's what I saw. Saw it plenty times. And Joe was J. Stalin, Group Captain, remember that, Joseph Stalin. And you guys in the R.A.F. wanted him for king. How do you explain that, if you aren't all commies?"

"I assure you," Mandrake said faintly, "it was just a joke. You know, people in the Royal Air Force sometimes have a strange sense of humor."

Ripper's mood abruptly changed. He smiled at Mandrake and said affectionately, "Well now, Group Captain, I can understand that. Some people say I have a strange sense of humor myself."

THE WAR ROOM

President Muffley had thought at length about the information he had been given by Turgidson and other advisers. He made his decision. "Get Premier Kissof on the 'Hot-Line'!"

As Staines picked up a phone and spoke into it, the President began to give orders to various aides. He ordered a complete communications system set up between the Pentagon and the Kremlin. It included a dozen telephone circuits, radios, and teleprinters. He gave the orders fast and decisively, brushing aside an objection that maintenance and installation men might not be on duty at that hour of the morning in Washington.

"So get them out of bed," he snapped, then turned to General Turgidson, who had again risen to his feet.

General Buck Turgidson was feeling confident. The President, he thought, could hardly deny the logic of what he was about to say. He knew that the President would probably not sympathize with his views. Privately Turgidson considered the President altogether too soft with the commies. But he was bound to agree with the rightness of Turgidson's views on subsequent action.

He smiled his usual preliminary smile and began.

"One: Our hopes for recalling the planes are quickly being reduced to a very low order of probability. Two: In less than fifteen minutes the Russkies will be making radar contacts with them. Three: When they do, they will go absolutely *ape* and strike back with everything they've got. Four: If prior to this we've done nothing further to suppress their retaliatory capabilities, we will suffer virtual annihilation. I believe our recent studies of this contingency indicated in round numbers upwards of a hundred and fifty million killed in the United States. Five: If, on the other hand, we *immediately* launch a co-ordinated and all-out missile attack on their airfields and missile bases, we stand a damned good chance of catching them with their pants down. Hell, we've got a five-to-one missile superiority and we can easily assign three missiles per target and still have a very effective reserve force for any other contingencies. Six: An unofficial study which we undertook of such an eventuality indicated we would destroy ninety per cent of their nuclear capabilities. We would therefore prevail and suffer only modest and acceptable civilian casualties from their remaining force, which would be badly damaged and completely lack the degree of co-ordination necessary for a decent and balanced striking force."

General Turgidson remained standing and smiled confidently at the President. The force of his argument must surely convince the President of the only possible policy for him to adopt, he thought.

President Muffley looked up. He said coldly, "General Turgidson, it is an avowed policy of our country that we will never strike first with nuclear weapons."

"Yes," General Turgidson said, "but don't you agree General Ripper has already invalidated that policy?"

"That was not an act of national policy," President Muffley said angrily. "It was done without my authority and there are still alternatives open to us. You say that there is a difference between striking first and pre-empting a Russian first strike, which you feel certain will be coming. But even if we struck first we would still suffer horrible civilian casualties."

"Well now," Turgidson said, "I'm not saying we wouldn't get our hair mussed, Mister President, but I do say not more than ten to twenty million dead depending on the breaks."

"General, you're talking about mass murder, not war."

"Mister President, we are rapidly approaching a moment of truth, for ourselves as human beings and for the life of our nation. Truth is not always a pleasant thing, but it is necessary now to make a choice. To choose between two admittedly regrettable but nevertheless distinguishable post-war environments—one where we lose twenty million people, and the other where we lose one hundred and fifty million people."

President Muffley said, "I do not intend to go down in history as the greatest mass murderer since Adolf Hitler."

General Turgidson's smile disappeared. He said quickly, "Perhaps it might be better, Mister President, if you concerned yourself more about the American people than your image in history books."

Turgidson's last speech was too much for the President to take. His headache was worse, and the necessity of dealing with people like Turgidson made it no better. He slammed his fist on the table and said, "General Turgidson, I think we've heard from you sufficiently on this." He glared at the General, who slowly sank down into his seat and then ostentatiously picked up a telephone and began to talk into it rapidly.

The President watched him for a moment, then turned aside to Staines. He said, "Find out what's happening with that call to the Premier."

Staines, glancing at the Big Board as he went, crossed the room to the guarded door. He opened it and went out of the War Room.

President Muffley looked again at Turgidson, who was still talking rapidly into his telephone, and then addressed Admiral Randolph. "I think I'd like a few more opinions. How about you, Admiral, do you agree with the General?"

Admiral Randolph, a neat and precise man, trimly dressed in gold-braided naval uniform, was visibly embarrassed by the President's question. He shook his head doubtfully and said, "I don't know... I just don't know."

Staines came back into the room and quietly slid into his seat near the President, who looked at him inquiringly. Staines said, "They're working on it, but no positive news yet."

The President acknowledged Staines's message, then turned to the representative of the Central Intelligence Agency, Bill Stover. "Bill, how about it?"

Stover replied without hesitation. "It's a difficult one, all right, but I guess I'll have to go along with your thinking, Mister President."

The President now looked at the Army Chief of Staff, General Faceman.

Faceman said slowly, "I see what General Turgidson's getting at, but it's rough." He paused and rubbed his large hand over his face, which he had not had time to shave before he came to the War Room. Then he said, "I'll just have to pass on this one, Mister President."

Staines picked up one of his phones in response to the quiet but unmistakable tone of its buzzer. He listened for thirty seconds to the agitated voice at the other end, then covered the speaker of the phone with his hand. He said, "Mister President, they've got the Ambassador waiting upstairs."

"Good, good. Any difficulty?"

Staines replied, "They say he's having a fit about that squad of military police."

President Muffley dismissed the matter as unimportant with a cutting motion of his hand. "It can't be helped," he said. "Have him brought down here right away."

Staines spoke rapidly into the telephone.

General Buck Turgidson jumped up again. "Mister President, is that the Russian Ambassador you're talking about? Are you actually going to let him into the War Room?"

The President inclined his head. "That is correct, General. He is here on my orders."

Turgidson said gravely, "Well, sir, I don't know quite how to put this, but are you aware what a serious breach of security that would be, I mean, he'll see everything." He gestured dramatically toward the central display, where the tracks of the encroaching bombers had now moved appreciably farther. "I mean, he'll see the Big Board."

President Muffley looked at Turgidson without affection. But his voice was patient. "That is precisely the idea, General," he said. "That is precisely the idea."

Strangelove pondered this. He was of course familiar with the jargon of the nuclear strategists. Indeed, he himself had created a great deal of it. He decided, for the moment, to say nothing. Later he would have an opportunity to speak, but at this time his acute brain was fully concentrated on watching the changing displays which were recording the progress of the bombers, as well as the increasing Russian air and submarine threat.

LEPER COLONY

Inside *Leper Colony*, heading in toward enemy territory, the crew had reached the stage of preparation at which the major task of arming the two weapons was necessary.

Lieutenant Lothar Zogg, the bombardier, received the word from King and depressed one of his master switches. He noted the light that winked on and said, "Bomb-arming circuits are green."

King nodded with satisfaction. He was like a fighter, eagerly anticipating a fight he knew he was going to win, who had reached the point where his handlers were beginning to tape his hands. This was the essential preliminary to combat. They had done it many times on training missions, and in synthetic trainers on the ground at Burpelson. But this was for real. This was it! King said happily, "Okay, Dietrich, you all right back there?"

Dietrich's voice was calm and confident. "Right, King."

The actual arming of the bombs, which converted them from inert masses of metal into the most potent of lethal weapons, required action by three separate crew members. Naturally King, as command pilot, was one. Lothar Zogg, as bombardier, was another. And Lieutenant Dietrich was the third. This was another safety device which had been built into the bomber, an example of cautious planning which insured that no single person could, through some unbalanced decision, start a war on his own.

King said crisply, "Primary arming switch."

Dietrich repeated the order and simultaneously he and King depressed a switch on the bomb-arming equipment each of them had in front of him. The switch, guarded by a safety trip, was marked number one.

On the bombardier's control panel two green lights glowed. Lothar Zogg depressed his own switch. He looked sideways and grinned at Sweets Kivel who was taking an intelligent interest in the procedure. Zogg said, "Primary circuit is live."

"All right, then," King said, "primary trigger switch."

As before, Dietrich repeated the order, and he and King both depressed their switches. Two more green lights glowed on Zogg's control panel. He depressed his own trigger switch, and a third green light appeared. He said, "Primary trigger switch is live. Shows three greens."

Lieutenant Dietrich's part in the arming was now finished. He played absently with the tuning control of his main radar while he listened to the remainder of the procedure carried out by King and Lothar Zogg.

Zogg said, "Release first safety."

They both operated their switches. Two lights again glowed on the safety bank of the panel. The same procedure was repeated for the second safety device. On the safety bank a second pair of lights came on. Only one pair now remained unlit.

It was now necessary to fuse the bombs so they would detonate at the required altitudes. Since they had two targets, it was standard operating procedure that the primary bomb was set first; but in this case, since their secondary target was close to the primary, King ordered both bombs to be fused at once.

Lothar Zogg said, "Fusing for impact, delay as briefed." He reached forward and turned the knob-setting of the altitude burst controller. The needle crept round the dial to the figure ten, and Zogg pressed in succession three control buttons which gave electronic, barometric, and time setting to the bomb fuses. Again this was a safety precaution, though of a slightly different nature. It was unlikely that any two of the fusing devices would fail at the same time and almost impossible that all three would fail.

The three lights told Zogg that all the fusing circuits were live. He pushed back his hair and said, "Master safety."

King leaned forward and pressed the last remaining switch on the panel, clearly marked "Master Safety." The two remaining lights on the safety panel shone, and Zogg glanced quickly along the banked rows of glowing lights.

He said, "Bombs are live and fused. All circuits are showing green."

King said, "Arming drill check."

Lothar repeated the drill mechanically as he checked the switches and lights of his equipment. "Bomb-fusing master safeties on. Electronic, barometric, time and impact. Fuse for ground burst, three minutes delay. Bomb circuits one through four, test lights on. Bomb-door circuits, test lights on. Bomb fusing green one through four, test lights on. Detonator set to zero altitude. Systems selector to ground burst three. Air-burst barometric-fusing-compensator cutout positive. Emergency power lights on. Auto/manual circuit live, first safety. Track indicators to maximum deflection. Primary trigger switch over ride engaged. Second safety, bombs alive. Arming drill check completed."

King said absently, "What was that, Lothar?" While Lothar had been speaking, his attention had been distracted by the portraits of his ancestors. The drill was routine. They had been through it many times before, and he knew that Dietrich was monitoring the checks.

Lothar Zogg repeated, "Arming drill check completed."

King said, "That's great, Zoggy. I acknowledge, arming drill check complete."

Below them in the cavernous bomb bay of the airplane *Hi-There* and *Lolita* waited. They were live now, and ready to go.

King was determined they *would* go.

BURPELSON AIR FORCE BASE

Dawn was slowly pushing a pale light over the vast base.

All around the wire perimeter fence, defense teams were in position, armed with carbines, rifles, machine guns and bazookas. They commanded all the approaches to the base, and they had with them adequate stores of ammunition and rations. In the distance was heard the first sound of rumbling truck engines. Not all the defense teams heard the noise; some of them were five miles away on the other side of the base. But many heard it, and in those positions men became alert, machine guns were cocked and swung in the direction from which the noise was coming.

The defense team commanded by Sergeant Mellows, who was searching the road with binoculars, suddenly detected in the uncertain light a jeep and three troop carriers approaching their defense position. The approach was slow and cautious.

Private Anderson, peering through the sights of his machine gun, said, "How do we know they're saboteurs?"

The sergeant rested his binoculars on his chest for a moment. He said coldly, "How do you know they're not?"

Corporal Engelbach, manning the bazooka, said, "That's right. You heard the General, Anderson. Two hundred yards, that's as near as we let them. And they're still coming closer."

Sergeant Mellows, who had been traversing his binoculars to cover the entire field of fire, said, "Hey, look! There's eight more trucks on the north road."

Engelbach turned to Anderson. "They have to be saboteurs. Who else would be coming at four in the morning?"

Anderson said, "Yeah, I guess so." He aligned his sights on the lead jeep.

Sergeant Mellows watched the approach of the vehicle calmly. Already they had set up a range indicator, which was a tall post at the side of the approach road. The four vehicles crept slowly toward it. Mellows said, "Any moment now."

Though the approach of the assault forces was slow, there was a certain massive implacability about it. Mellows wondered just how many men were in the four vehicles they were covering and the eight on the north road. He watched the lead jeep reach the range marker and roll on past it.

He said quietly, in the way he had been taught at N.C.O. School, "Okay, let them have it."

Anderson had the lead jeep clearly in his sights. He pressed the trigger of the machine gun, held it for five seconds, released it, and then fired twice more. Instantly the convoy stopped and men erupted from the jeep, running desperately for cover from the lethal stream of bullets.

Corporal Engelbach fired his bazooka and grunted with satisfaction as he scored a direct hit with his first shot. The empty jeep exploded violently, and its broken, shattered parts burned fiercely.

In the light of the flames from the jeep, men were seen hurriedly leaping out of the three trucks which had followed the jeep and disappearing rapidly into the fields on each side of the road. These were men of a crack outfit. They were highly battle-trained, and many of them were battle-experienced too, veterans of Okinawa and Korea and other places in Asia where the cold war had at certain times become hotter than hot. They were experienced under fire, and soon they were pouring it into the defense positions, sending flails of lead splashing across the top of the positions.

All around the perimeter of the base violent fire fights were developing. They would become sporadic in places, even die away completely as each side cautiously probed for the location of the other. Then they would break out again, and the night became a hideous medley of the crack of carbines, the heavy drumming of machine guns, and the powerful thud of bazookas and mortar shells.

The commander of the assault troops spoke into his walkie-talkie. He gave an order. Gradually the firing died down, and in the silence that followed, the noise of the night insects was heard again.

On both sides men peered anxiously into the gray light, looking for targets. But these were difficult to find.

The noise of the insects was stilled momentarily by the metallic click of a loudspeaker. Behind one of the trucks which had been brought to a stop by Sergeant Mellows' defense team the commander of the assault troops began to talk into the loudspeaker equipment.

He said, his voice loud and clear, "Men, this is Colonel Guano, commanding an airborne division of the United States Army. Why are you firing at us?"

There was silence on the base. Guano waited thirty seconds, then clicked on his speaker and repeated his message.

In the defense position Private Anderson turned to look at Sergeant Mellows. He said, "Hey, he sounds real American. Don't we answer?"

Mellows looked at Anderson with scorn. "You jest keep your head down and open up on the first one of them shows theirs."

Guano tried again. "This is Colonel Guano. I repeat, Colonel Guano. We're on a mission from the President. We want to enter the base and speak with General Ripper."

Again there was silence. Corporal Engelbach said musingly, "A special mission from the President, what do you know about that?"

Sergeant Mellows was still looking intently through his binoculars. He said, "I know one thing. You've got to give these Reds credit for great organization and planning."

Two hundred yards away a skirmishing party of a dozen men, widely spaced out with about thirty yards between each man, rose out of the grass and began to work its way forward.

Anderson said quietly, "And plenty guts, too." He looked carefully through his sights and began to fire on the skirmish line. He traversed the machine gun rapidly and in the first burst three men were hit. The others immediately dived for cover and became invisible to Anderson in the concealment of the tall grass.

From the cover of the truck Colonel Guano had watched the progress of the party. His instructions were that he should not open fire unless he was refused admittance to the base, but there had been little time to brief his troops adequately, and in his opinion they had been justified in returning the fire which had poured into them from the defense positions. But now there was a break in the firing and Guano decided he must make one last effort to gain admittance without taking any further casualties.

He spoke through his loudspeaker. "This is Colonel Guano. Men, you are firing on your own troops. Unless you surrender within sixty seconds I am under orders to return your fire with everything I've got and forcibly penetrate your base." He clicked off the speaker and waited for some response.

Sergeant Mellows said softly to Engelbach, "That's okay by me, comrade," pointed his carbine at the truck, and let loose five rapid shots. Anderson also opened up with his machine gun.

Bullets zipped close to Colonel Guano and the company commanders who were with him. Guano turned to his company commanders. He said, "They must all be crazy! What the hell's going on?"

He thought for a moment, then made his decision. "All right, Johnson. Take C Company round to the flank." He indicated the direction with his hand. Johnson moved off.

Then Guano turned to the other two company commanders, Rothman and Cooper, and quickly gave them their instructions. They too moved off.

Guano's deployment was quickly seen from the base, and the defense positions opened fire. But Guano's soldiers were highly skilled in this type of mission, and though they lost men, they still moved forward.

LEPER COLONY

The bomber was down to twenty thousand feet as it approached the coast.

Lieutenant Sweets Kivel was hunched over his search radarscope, which he had adjusted to short range to get a clear definition of the point they would cross. This was important, both to get a completely accurate navigation fix, and also to evade predicted flak defenses. He checked the radar picture against his map, then said, "We should be crossing the coast in about six minutes. We're on track. It looks good."

King said, "Thanks, Sweets." He looked ahead toward the enemy coast but could not yet see it.

Lieutenant Dietrich was also hunched over his radarscope. But this was not navigational radar; it was search radar designed to detect enemy missiles and fighters.

Dietrich suddenly saw a blip appear on the scope. He watched it closely, then said, "Missile! Sixty miles off, heading in fast, steady track—looks like a beam-rider."

King reacted with the assurance of a veteran. He said, "Awright, keep callin'!"

Then he turned to Ace Owens. "Knock off the auto-pilot, Ace."

Ace reached forward and flipped the two switches. He said, "Autopilot off."

King said crisply, "Lock ECM to master search radar."

Dietrich reacted immediately. He flipped the switches and made the necessary adjustments in tuning. He said, "ECM locked to master search radar."

In front of him the large electronic counter-measures control panel was functioning perfectly. He gave it an approving pat. Well now, he thought, this is it. He adjusted the scope again and carefully measured with a strobe marker the range of the enemy missile.

Ace Owens said, "Where do you suppose it's coming from?"

King looked at his altimeter and frowned. They still had too much height. He considered the possibilities of evading the missile. At this height they were not good, and they were not going to get down to a safe height before the missile arrived.

He said, "Dietrich, you picked up any fighters?"

Dietrich shook his head. He said, "Just the missile."

King thought about the situation again. He fitted into place all the assessments he had studied from intelligence reports. He said slowly, "It must of been fired from Brombingna Island, probably that there new Vampire two-o-two, the one with a hundred-mile range."

Dietrich broke in on him, "Forty-five. Straight and fast. Coming in at twelve o'clock."

"What speed?"

"Between Mach three and four."

"Call it every five miles."

"Thirty-five, it's still coming!"

King made his decision. "Prepare to release Quail."

Bombardier Lothar Zogg flipped a number of switches and checked that the circuits were in good shape. He said, "Quail ready for release."

"Open bomb doors."

Lothar Zogg said immediately, "Bomb doors are open."

King acknowledged the message. He thought he would wait until the last moment before releasing Quail. He considered that time would come when the missile was between thirty and twenty-five miles away. It would only be a few seconds now until he had to decide to give the executive order.

They carried only one Quail decoy, designed to divert enemy radar and missiles. It was a decision of great importance.

Dietrich called, "Thirty! Twelve o'clock and straight!"

King decided. He said calmly, "Release Quail."

The decoy dropped from the bomb bay. It fell a few feet, and then a jet flame appeared as it came to life.

King acknowledged Lothar Zogg's message that the decoy had been released. He said calmly, "Changing course ninety degrees. Close bomb doors."

Zogg said, "Bomb doors closed."

Dietrich's voice was excited, high pitched. "Twenty miles, heading in straight."

King banked the huge airplane, and watched the gyros carefully as they altered.

Below the bomber, as it turned, the Quail decoy turned also, duplicating the bomber's alteration of course. It was about a hundred yards beneath the B-52.

Lothar Zogg looked at his radarscope. He said quickly, "Something must be wrong. Quail turned with us."

Immediately King straightened out of the turn and banked the airplane the other way. He said, "Changing course ninety degrees."

Dietrich called the missile at fifteen miles and twelve o'clock.

Again the Quail missile turned with the bomber and Lothar Zogg detected the turn on his radarscope. He said, "It's still following us."

As Lothar finished speaking, Dietrich called the missile at ten miles, still heading in straight.

Again, King had to make a decision. The electronic brain installed in *Leper Colony* was the product of years of patient research by the greatest experts in the field. But apparently it was not powerful enough to divert the enemy missile. There was more power available, but also there was the possibility of blowing the set. It was a risk that had to be taken.

King said, "Okay, take the ECM over the red line."

Dietrich made the adjustments to the set. He turned it to maximum power and the power gauges instantly showed their arrows quivering past the red line.

Dietrich said, "Maximum power. It's at eight miles."

Lothar Zogg, looking intently into his radarscope, said, "Quail is with us. Looks like it's going to follow us whatever we do."

Beads of sweat were now forming on King's face, but he was still very well in command.

He said, "Hang on, boys," and flipped the plane into a series of violent turns to get away from Quail.

Lothar Zogg, watching his radarscope, continued to report that the decoy was following them.

Dietrich said, "Seven miles."

King pushed forward violently on the controls.

Dietrich said, "Six."

Lothar Zogg said, "Still with us."

"Five miles."

King pulled back on the controls. It was now, he thought, that a sudden climb might throw off the missile.

Dietrich said, "Four miles."

King watched the instruments as the bomber checked its descent, then began to rise. He called for maximum engine power, and Captain Ace Owens adjusted the throttles to give it.

Lothar Zogg said, "Keeping right with us."

Dietrich said, "Two miles, heading right in."

King frowned. This wasn't right. The ECM should have made the missile break off. He pulled back harder on the controls to make the climb steeper.

Beneath the bomber the malfunctioning Quail decoy

followed as faithfully as a favored puppy. Something had gone wrong with its guidance system, and it was locked on to the bomber which had released it.

Dietrich called, "Coming in to minimum range."

The Russian missile was still climbing when it approached *Leper Colony*. The beam which had directed it was too diffuse at this range for it to sense the difference between the bomber and the decoy. Its guidance system picked up Quail, and the missile closed on the decoy.

One hundred yards below *Leper Colony* there was a huge explosion as missile and decoy collided.

The airplane bucked violently as the blast wave of the explosion hit. King fought to control it, his vision impeded by the thick smoke that filled the pressurized area of the plane.

He said, "Everyone on emergency oxygen. Guess we've been hit somewheres. I'm takin' her down on the deck."

He pushed the controls forward and again *Leper Colony* slid down toward the enemy coast. The controls were operating normally, King decided. He checked them, then called for damage reports from the crew. He received them from all except one crew member, repeated his request, then leaned across and jerked his elbow into Ace Owens' ribs.

Ace turned his head slightly. He looked at King and his mouth opened to form a word. But the word did not come. His eyes closed and he slumped sideways in his seat.

THE WAR ROOM

On the main display the bomber tracks moved forward again. Ambassador De Sadeski watched their progress, then turned and spoke with furious intensity to the President. "You are very clever, Mister President! You send nuclear planes to destroy Russia! You call me in here and tell me the planes are coming but it is an *accident*. You say, 'do not strike back, Russia, this is an accident.' So the trusting people of the Soviet Union believe you? Sit back, and *bang*, you destroy us. Ha! Your trick is clever, Mister President, but one thing you forget—we are chess players, and in chess there are no tricks! No tricks, Mister President! Just traps! And only the beginner falls for traps. We are not beginners."

"Mister Ambassador, you are choosing to misunderstand."

"Understand? Understand? I understand only too well. Who could fail to understand such a clumsy trick? A trick!—at the expense of the peace-loving people of the Soviet Union. One...last...gigantic...trick!"

"Anger will not help us now, Mister Ambassador."

"Nothing will help you now, Mister President! We are not fooled by this fantastic lie! I am not fooled, and the Premier will not be fooled! We are not such fools as you may think, Mister President!"

President Muffley looked at De Sadeski in silence for a moment. He had known him for several years and knew also that De Sadeski was highly regarded by the power elite in the Kremlin. He gave a prearranged signal to one of his aides who hastened to the drinks table.

The President said, "Mister Ambassador, I have always had the greatest respect for your intelligence, for your shrewd judgment of character, and for your coolness and ability to handle a crisis. When I speak to the Premier, we must be able to authenticate what I tell him. Your presence here is perhaps the single most important hope we have to prevent a complete and final catastrophe, because you will be able to supply this authentication. That is why I brought you here and why I revealed our classified and highly guarded procedures."

De Sadeski sighed, but said nothing for a moment. He pondered the implications of the President's speech, looked up at the huge displays, and decided that at least it could do no harm to remain in this room while he had the opportunity. He respected the President's intelligence, if not his beliefs, and he was prepared to spend some time in finding out exactly what was in the President's mind and any other information he might acquire for later use.

The aide arrived bearing a silver tray on which stood a bottle of vodka and several full glasses. He offered the tray to De Sadeski. "Here you are, sir."

De Sadeski reached automatically for a glass, lifted it to his lips, then abruptly lowered it onto the table. He looked directly at the President. He said slowly and suspiciously, "You wouldn't put anything in it?"

The President did not bother to answer. He reached across, took the glass, and downed the shot of vodka in one gulp.

De Sadeski said, "Pardon me, but you will understand that I cannot be too cautious."

President Muffley breathed deeply, both to counteract the impact of the vodka and to keep a tight rein on his feelings. "Perhaps," he said stiffly, "this unfounded suspicion will better allow you to realize that your other suspicions are equally unfounded."

De Sadeski said nothing but reached for another glass and downed the liquor like water. Then he smacked his lips and nodded in appreciation.

The President relaxed in his chair. He said quietly, "Won't you have something to eat now? You must be feeling hungry and we may have a long wait down here."

The Ambassador considered the matter for a moment. He glanced across at the large and appetizing collection of food he could see on the long table. He was certainly feeling hungry, but at the same time considered that he ought not be too conciliatory. Finally he said, "Very well."

The aide was instantly at his elbow. He said deferentially, "Follow me, sir."

The Ambassador followed the aide to the long table. He walked up and down examining the display of food. There were dishes of all kinds, hot trays, cold cuts, and a profuse variety of drinks, both alcoholic and non-alcoholic. De Sadeski detected one item of food that was not there. He asked for it. "You don't have any fresh fish?"

The aide was embarrassed. He looked hastily along the table. "I'm afraid not, sir."

De Sadeski felt pleased with the point he had made. Now he could relax a little. He said, "Your eggs, then, they're fresh?"

"Naturally, sir."

"Then I will have poached eggs. And bring me some cigars, please—Havana cigars, of course."

Admiral Randolph had moved up close to De Sadeski and the aide. Now he produced a large and ornate cigar case which he offered to the Ambassador. "Try one of these Jamaican cigars, Mister Ambassador. I think you'll find they're pretty good."

De Sadeski ignored the case. He said coldly, "Thank you, no. I do not support the work of imperialist stooges."

Admiral Randolph stared at him in surprise. He snapped the case shut and turned away from De Sadeski, speaking over his shoulder as he went. "Only commie stoogies, huh?"

De Sadeski's face was impressive. He watched Randolph walk up to another officer, and heard him say, "Well, what the hell, Ed! Offer a guy a smoke and the lousy sonofa..."

De Sadeski heard no more, as the two officers walked away together to examine closely the display on which the deployment of Russian submarines was indicated. They were more numerous now as fresh detections were reported and flashed on to the display.

De Sadeski also examined the display thoughtfully. He glanced quickly round the room and saw that nobody seemed to be watching him. The aide was busy at the table, filling the order for poached eggs.

Some distance away from De Sadeski, General Buck Turgidson was speaking angrily to the President. Turgidson had overheard the conversation between the Ambassador and Admiral Randolph. He was saying, "Mister President, you gonna let that lousy commie punk vomit all over us that way?"

President Muffley had been annoyed by De Sadeski's remark. But unlike Turgidson he had the ability to repress his annoyance. He needed De Sadeski, and he also needed Turgidson, if they were to get some satisfactory answer to this mess. He said, "Look Buck, I know how you feel. How do you think I like it? Now cool off, there's a helluva lot riding on this phone call. Okay?"

"If you say so, sir."

"Good boy, Buck."

Turgidson turned away and picked up one of his telephones. He began to speak into it rapidly, at the same time noting that on the main display of the Big Board the bomber tracks had progressed farther toward their target. His crew-cut head bobbed vigorously as he emphasized a point. He was in fact talking to SAC, letting his old friend in command there know his feelings about the Russian Ambassador.

The President called Staines to his side. He said sharply, "What's taking so long on that call to Premier Kissof?"

Staines said, "Mister President, we haven't been able to reach him at the Kremlin. They say they don't know where he is, and he isn't expected back for another two hours."

"Did you tell them what I told you?"

"I was hoping it would not be necessary, sir."

Ambassador De Sadeski had moved up to them as they talked. He broke into the conversation. "You are having trouble reaching the Premier?"

"Yes, we are, Ambassador."

"On Saturday afternoon his office will not know where to find him. Try eighty-seven, forty-six, fifty-six, Moscow."

President Muffley said quickly, "Did you get that, Staines?" He waited for Staines to repeat the numbers then continued, "Get on to it right now."

Staines walked quickly away. The President said, "Thank you very much, Ambassador."

De Sadeski rubbed his fingers along the side of his nose. He said quietly but emphatically, "You will note that I recalled that number from memory, Mister President. I emphasize this because of what I said earlier about chess. You understand the importance of memory to the chess master?"

President Muffley inclined his head. "You have indeed an impressive memory, Ambassador."

"Thank you, Mister President." De Sadeski paused for

a moment to consider whether he ought to go on with what he had intended to say. On balance, he thought so. It was important, he felt, to convey clearly to the President that the Russian Premier shared the normal human emotions of people everywhere. He said, "You would never have found him through his office, of course. Our Premier is a man of the people. He is also a *man*, a man of *affairs*, if you follow my meaning."

Turgidson had replaced his telephone in time to hear what De Sadeski was saying. He turned to the officer on his right and said, "Degenerate, atheistic commie!"

De Sadeski overheard Turgidson's remark. He said furiously to the President, "I formally request that you have this...this...checker-player removed from the War Room."

President Muffley suppressed a groan. The situation was already highly explosive. But the obvious antagonism between Turgidson and the Ambassador was making it even more dangerous. He rapped a pencil down on the table and said sternly to Turgidson, "General, the Soviet Ambassador is here as my guest and is to be treated as such. You understand me?"

Turgidson's face was livid with anger. He was furious that the President should take the side of a lousy commie, even if he was their Ambassador, against himself. But the President by nature of his office was constitutionally Turgidson's Commander-in-Chief. It took a great effort, but he said, "If you say so, Mister President," and again picked up a telephone into which he began to talk rapidly.

The President became aware that Staines was signaling to him. He looked up in inquiry.

"Mister President, they're trying the number now."

The President rose to his feet and walked toward Staines.

Suddenly, before he had reached Staines's side, there was a tremendous commotion behind him. He swung around.

General Turgidson and Ambassador De Sadeski were grappling wildly on the floor, their limbs threshing and flailing as they fought, bumping into furnishings and knocking over a small table with a crash.

President Muffley hastily went toward them. He shouted, "Gentlemen! For the love of God! What's the meaning of this?"

Other officers had now approached the two struggling men. They saw the President's agitation and several of them physically separated the combatants, afterward helping them to their feet.

De Sadeski shrugged off the officers who had assisted him and immediately assumed a *karate* stance. He was puffing but defiant as he said, "So, General! You had not tasted karate before, eh?"

General Buck Turgidson clenched his fists. He said, "Why you commie punk, I'll knock that commie head right off your lousy commie neck."

President Muffley stepped between the two men.

De Sadeski did not relax his posture. He said, "Mister President, my Government shall hear of this personal attack and this attempt to discredit its Ambassador."

President Muffley said sharply, "Gentlemen, I demand an explanation!"

De Sadeski pointed. "You will find an explanation, Mister President, concealed in the right hand of this war-mongering bully."

Turgidson grinned. His face had a triumphant expression as he extended his hand toward the President. "You're not kidding there, Mister Commie. Here is the explanation, Mister President, in full!"

He opened his fist to reveal a tiny spy camera, which

had been disguised as a cigarette lighter. He went on. "This commie rat was using this thing to take pictures of the Big Board, and that is the explanation."

Ambassador De Sadeski said coldly, "Mister President, this clumsy fool tried to plant that ridiculous camera on me, actually tried to plant it! He tried to put it into my coat pocket, but a taste of karate changed his mind. *That* is the explanation."

Turgidson burst out, "That's a damned lie. I saw him with my own eyes."

De Sadeski shrugged his shoulders. He turned to the President, pointed to his torn side pocket and said, "Here is the evidence, look. He tried to plant it, but my karate sent him flying."

Turgidson's fists clenched again and he stepped forward. "Why you rotten, lying, commie punk, I'll…"

President Muffley said sharply, "Now stop this. Gentlemen, this has gone too far. You will stop it immediately."

Dr. Strangelove had been watching the startling interchange between the Ambassador and the General, his glasses hiding a look of cynical amusement. He turned, suddenly alert, as at that precise moment Staines's voice saved the situation.

He said excitedly, "Mister President, I think they're getting the Premier."

LEPER COLONY

King looked closely at Ace. He must have been hit, he decided. He shouted, "Hey, one of you guys come an' look to ole Ace here."

Dietrich left his seat and moved forward to the flight deck.

King checked his instruments. Fire-warning lights were glowing on engines three and four in the port inner pod. He said, "Shuttin' down three an' four," and flipped the switches.

The needles of the revolution indicators for three and four slowly swung to zero, and as fuel to the engines was cut, the fire died. But a wisp of smoke still trailed from the pod.

King said to the crew, "Awright, fire systems workin'."

The smoke was still thick inside the airplane. King could taste it, though he was on emergency oxygen. There was only one solution, he thought. They must get down to low level as fast as possible.

He trimmed the bomber for maximum rate descent and said, "I'm takin' her down on the deck. And I mean on the deck. Sweets, that okay?"

Sweets Kivel consulted his chart. "Sure, King, no high ground on track for a while yet."

The bomber slanted down in a deep descent. Dietrich, who was struggling to get Ace out of his seat, said, "Hey, I can't move him while she's going down. King, looks like he's hit in the shoulder. Maybe shock too," he added. Dietrich prided himself on his medical knowledge. He had completed one year of pre-med before entering the Air Force.

King said, "One of you guys come help. Lothar?"

"Yes, King?"

"You got any damage?"

Lothar Zogg checked again. He was satisfied it was all working right. He said, "No damage, King."

"Awright, come up here and help."

Lothar climbed up to the flight deck, and helped Dietrich to get Ace Owens out of his seat and back to the bunk which was used by crewmen when they needed rest.

King held the bomber steady in the steep descent. It was losing height at five thousand feet a minute now. He looked at the fuel gauges and saw that several of them were swinging erratically. Probably, he thought, because the descent was so steep.

Dietrich said, "We got Ace on the bunk, King. He just opened his eyes. I don't think he's hit too bad."

"Great," King said, and looked again at the fuel gauges. Then he continued, "Listen, Dietrich, you fix him up with a dressing for the wound, then get back on that set. I want everything we got blasting out jamming when we get down on the deck."

"Roger, King."

King concentrated on his instruments, saw everything was normal, then asked the crew for damage reports.

Sweets Kivel said, "All my stuff is working fine, but say, King, there's one little thing I'm worried about."

"What's that?"

"Well, your fuel gauges acting like mine are? Kind of jumping around?"

King looked at his gauges again. The needles were still oscillating, but less than before. He said, "Lemme worry about that, kid. We're still flyin' and that's the way it's gonna be. Goldy, how about it? You got any trouble?"

Lieutenant Goldberg's voice was excited. He said, "Well, King, haven't finished my check yet. Tell you one thing, though, there's a big hole in the side of the plane right opposite the CWIE. I'm checking it out."

King accepted this without comment and said, "Dietrich, you back on station yet?"

Dietrich was sliding into his seat as King's message came through. Goldberg pointed to the flight deck and Dietrich hastily connected his intercom.

King said, "Dietrich, you hear me?"

"Yeah, sure, King."

"So how's Ace?"

"Not bad, King," Dietrich said quickly. "It ain't a bad wound. He'll maybe survive."

"I'm glad to hear it. Right glad to hear it. You look after ole Ace. Now you hear me?"

"Sure, King."

"Awright, now check your equipment."

"Roger, King." Dietrich looked at his ECM. He tested the circuits, found them working well.

He said, "All circuits tested and good. You want emergency power when we're on the deck, King?"

" Will it help?"

"Sure it'll help—jam out everything in radar range of us. See, down on the deck we need the extra power, too much interference, you know trees and hills and stuff. It'll help."

King said, "So use it. We aim to make that target, an' we gonna make it. So use every damn thing you need. Ain't nothin' to stop us if we go in at low level."

"Okay," Dietrich said, "I'll keep it high as I think will be safe."

"You do that."

King made himself more comfortable in his seat. He thought briefly of Ace Owens, then forgot him as he watched for the enemy coast.

There were many dangers ahead, he knew. High ground not shown on the combat maps, fighters, ground-to-air missiles, flak. But he had been trained to deal with these. He knew that a plane barreling along at about six hundred knots was almost invulnerable to the defenses if it was down on the deck. And that was where he intended to take *Leper Colony*.

He said, "I'm settin' for maximum speed at deck level."

Sweets replied immediately. "You know what that'll do to our fuel consumption?"

"Can't be hepped. What kinda wind we got, Sweets?"

"The wind might help. Looks to be going our way. But my guess is, if we use maximum speed we're going to have to paddle our way back."

King said, "Well, we'll worry about that when the time comes."

He looked ahead and saw the enemy coast.

BURPELSON AIR FORCE BASE

Inside General Ripper's office, the marks of combat were showing. Occasional bursts of automatic fire had blasted into the room, into the walls, and across the pictures and decorations which hung on the walls. Now they were damaged and twisted, and the floor of the room was littered with pieces of wallboard and broken glass.

Ripper and Mandrake sat protected by the General's desk. Their glasses were beside them on the carpet, and Ripper was nursing a 30-caliber Browning air-cooled machine gun across his knees.

His expression was determined, and as he listened to the noise of the fighting out on the base, he nodded with approval. He said, "The boys are doing good, Group Captain. Real good."

"Why yes," Mandrake said, "they certainly are." He ducked involuntarily as another burst of fire crashed into the room.

Ripper raised his glass, drank slowly, and said, "Group Captain Mandrake, have you ever seen a Russian drink a glass of water?"

"No, sir, I don't believe I ever have."

"Vodka. That's what they drink, isn't it? Never water."

"Well, I—I can't really say, sir."

"On no account will a Russian ever drink water, and not without good reason."

Mandrake looked at Ripper anxiously. He could not understand this emphasis on fluid and water. But Ripper appeared to be perfectly composed. Mandrake said, "I'm afraid I don't quite see what you're getting at, sir."

Ripper removed his cigar from his mouth and waved it at Mandrake. "Water! That's what I'm getting at, *water!* Water is the source of all life. Four-fifths of the surface of the earth is water, ninety-eight per cent of the human body is water. As human beings we require fresh, pure water to replenish our precious bodily fluids. Are you beginning to understand, Group Captain?"

"No, sir, I'm afraid I can't say that I am."

"Have you never wondered why I drink only distilled water, or rain water, and only pure grain alcohol?"

Mandrake said, "Yes, sir, I have wondered—yes."

Ripper looked at his empty glass gloomily. He held it out to Mandrake, who scrambled on his knees across the floor for a refill.

Ripper said, "Have you ever heard of a thing called fluoridation, Group Captain, fluoridation of water?"

Mandrake paused to consider the question, then replied, "Yes, I think so, sir. Isn't that something that has to do with teeth? I mean, isn't it supposed to keep you from getting cavities or something like that?"

Again a burst of fire splashed across the room. Mandrake crawled back to Ripper.

The general said, "That sounded close. Now you just help me with this machine gun, Group Captain. Feed the belt of ammunition to me as I fire. There's some joker outside our window pouring it in."

He cocked the gun with a jerk of his powerful hands, fed the first cartridge into the breech, and worked the cocking device again. "Here we go," he said, stood up and advanced toward the window, with Mandrake crouching beside him ready to help the ammunition feed into the gun.

The general instantly saw the target he had been seeking, where a sniper had positioned himself on the building opposite the office. He opened fire, his massive form vibrating as the heavy machine gun bucked and kicked in his hands. Mandrake, still crouching, held the ammunition belt straight to feed the rounds into the gun. The noise inside the office was deafening as Ripper fired burst after burst, and soon the carpet was littered thickly with empty bullet cases.

Ripper ceased firing for a moment, stared out through the shuttered windows, then put in another long burst. Again he ceased fire and said to Mandrake with satisfaction, "That's done it. I got him." They both sat down on the floor and Ripper picked up his glass with his right hand while still clutching the machine gun with his left.

He said, "Like I was saying, Group Captain, fluoridation of water is the most monstrously conceived and dangerous communist plot we have ever had to face.

The fluorides form a basis of insecticides, fungicides, and rodent poisons. They pollute our precious bodily fluids! They clog them, Group Captain! Our precious bodily fluids become thick and rancid."

Mandrake said thoughtfully, "Well, sir, I should have thought the scientists had checked it. At least that's what one reads."

Ripper smiled. "Precisely, Group Captain. In order to realize the fantastic extent of communist infiltration, one has only to count the number of scientists, educators, public health officials, congressmen and senators who are behind it. *The facts are all there*, Group Captain!"

Ripper leaned his machine gun against the desk and crawled over to a drawer. He opened it and pulled out a thick file. As he crept back to where Mandrake sat, a burst of automatic fire splattered across the wall. But Ripper was oblivious to it.

He said, "I have studied the facts carefully for over seventeen years, and they're all here." He tapped the file. "I have watched this thing grow since the end of World War Two to the incredible proportions it has reached today. I have studied the facts, Group Captain, *facts*, and by projecting the statistics I realized the time had come to act. I realized I *had* to act before the entire will and vitality of the free Western world was sapped and polluted and clotted and made rancid by this diabolical substance, *fluoride*. The absolutely fantastic thing is that the facts are all there for anyone who wants to see them. Do you know any facts about fluorides, Group Captain Mandrake?"

Mandrake stroked his mustache. He said, "Well, not actually, sir." Outside, the sound of firing was heavier now. It seemed to Mandrake that it was getting closer too.

Ripper patted Mandrake's shoulder with his big hand.

He said affectionately, "You're a good officer, Group Captain. Loyal. From here on in you do not call me sir, you understand. You call me Jack, and that's an order."

Mandrake looked uneasy. Things like this simply did not happen in the Royal Air Force. But an order was an order. He gulped some of his drink and said, "I understand...Jack."

Ripper said, "That's right. That's my name. Jack." He listened attentively to the sounds of firing outside, then turned to Mandrake again. "And those are my boys out there. They're fighting. They're dying for me, you know that."

"And I'm sure they're proud and pleased to do it," Mandrake said warmly, "every man jack of them, er, Jack."

"I'm glad to hear you say that," Ripper said. "What were we talking about?"

"Well actually you were asking me if I knew any facts about fluorides."

Ripper inclined his massive head. "Well now," he said, "the facts are simple. Fluorine belongs to the halogen group, that is group seven of the period tables. It is the most active of all elements. It is transmitted from the mother to the foetus through the placenta, and it is also present in the breast milk. It is also found in the human body in bones, teeth, thyroid, hair, liver, kidneys, skin, nails, wool, feathers, horns, hooves and scales."

Mandrake looked at the general closely. Ripper's face was calm and reposed, but a small tic was apparent under his left eye. He said, "Yes, Jack, I see."

Then Ripper went on. "Group Captain, I have been following this thing very carefully for years, ever since the commies introduced it. The facts are all there if anyone takes the trouble to study them. Did you know that in addition to fluoridating water there are studies under way to fluoridate salt, flour, fruit juices, soup, sugar, milk, and ice cream! *Ice cream*, Group Captain. *Children's* ice cream! Do you know when fluoridation first began, Group Captain?"

"No, I can't say that I do, Jack."

Ripper removed his cigar from his mouth and carefully inspected the glowing tip. He said slowly, "It began in 1946. You see the significance?"

Mandrake said, "Well…"

Ripper went on. "Nineteen forty-six, Group Captain. How does that coincide with the postwar communist conspiracy? Incredibly obvious, isn't it? A foreign substance is introduced into the precious bodily fluids, without the knowledge of the individual and certainly without any free choice. That's the way the commies work…"

Mandrake thought about it for a moment. Then he said, "Jack, can I ask you a question?"

Ripper waved his cigar in a magnanimous gesture. "Sure, Group Captain, you're a good officer."

"Jack, when did you first develop this, er, theory about fluoridation?"

Ripper said, "It's *not* a theory. It is an awareness of an absolute certainty."

"Yes, I see that Jack, but when did you first become aware of this?"

Ripper appeared not to have heard the question. He was staring at the opposite wall. Mandrake repeated the question.

Ripper's eyes slowly turned toward Mandrake. He said, "Have you ever loved a woman, Group Captain? Physically loved her?"

Mandrake had no chance to reply before Ripper went on. "There's a feeling of loss, a profound sense of emptiness. Luckily, however, I was able to interpret the signs correctly. It was a loss of essence. But I can assure you it has not recurred, Group Captain. Women sense my power, and they seek me out. I do not avoid women, Group Captain." His voice became louder. "But I deny them my life essence."

Mandrake chewed thoughtfully on his mustache. He did not know what to say to the general, who had resumed his survey of the wall. He was saved from any necessity to reply by a sudden silence which had fallen over the base. He had been aware during the past few minutes that firing was sputtering out, and now it had finally ceased.

Ripper became aware of it too. He crossed to the window and looked out through the shattered blinds. In the distance he saw a squad of soldiers marching a party of base security troops, weaponless and with their hands clasped over their heads, into a hangar. He turned away from the window. Mandrake moved over toward him. Ripper's face was ravaged, the face of a man grown suddenly old. The tic beneath his left eye was more pronounced now. He said, "They've surrendered."

LEPER COLONY

King finished the descent and looked out at the terrain passing underneath them. There was snow on the ground, and on both sides of them there were peaks much higher than they were.

But Sweets Kivel had navigated accurately. The high ground was not in front of them. King concentrated on flying the bomber, determined he would take it through to the target. He said, "You got the next headin', Sweets?"

Lieutenant Kivel looked down at his chart, picked up his computer and began to figure. He said, "Yeah, King, one-eight-four." He busied himself with the computer again.

King said, "Hey, Dietrich, how's Ace doin' back there—and how's the ECM?"

Dietrich said, "Both doing great, King." He looked at the ECM panel, made small adjustments, then said, "ECM in good shape, King. Goldberg's going to see Ace."

Goldberg left his seat and moved forward to Ace's bunk.

Ace looked up at him. "How you doing, Goldy?"

"I'm fine," Goldberg said. "And you, Ace?"

Ace said, "I'm okay, Goldy."

Goldberg leaned over and dabbed the sweat on Ace's forehead with his clean handkerchief. Ace closed his eyes and snuggled down in the bunk to go to sleep.

Goldberg watched him for a second, then went back to his position. He talked on the intercom to King. "King, are you there?"

"Now, Goldy," King said, "where in hell did ya think I'd be? Sure I'm here, you jest tell me what's on your mind."

Lieutenant Goldberg said, "King, I just looked at Ace. He don't look too good. But I think he'll live."

"Well, that's fine, because he's comin' with us on the biggest thing ever. On a *nu-clear* strike against the Russkies."

Goldberg said, "Okay, King, whatever you say." He turned back to the bunk where Ace lay, reached forward, and touched him on the head.

Ace Owens said, "Thanks, Goldy, you're a pal."

Lieutenant Goldberg stood for a second, then turned and went back to his position in front of the shattered radio. He said, "Like I told you, I don't think we'll get much out of this. Maybe I'm wrong, but I don't think so."

King, who was concentrating on pushing the bomber in over the coast, had time to reply to Goldberg. He said, "Whaddya mean, Goldy, where's the trouble?"

Goldberg said, "King, I'm telling you the radio is out. I can't repair it, and I think it won't be any more use."

Goldberg switched off his microphone and looked down at the graphs which detailed the radio frequencies of the planes entering Russia and the defenses they would have to encounter. He switched on his microphone again and said, "All checks are made on ECM procedures."

THE WAR ROOM

The buzz of chatter among the officers and officials in the War Room suddenly ceased. Staines's voice came clearly, and was heard by them all. "Mister President, they've got the Premier on the line. His interpreter is with him. He'll shoot a simultaneous translation from you to the Premier, and vice versa."

The President took a deep breath and held out his hand for the phone. Around the table the group hastily took their seats and twenty-three hands reached for twenty-three extension phones.

The President said, "Hello? Hello? Dimitri, is this you?" He paused for the answer then went on. "Yes, this is Merkin, how are you?"

This time the pause was longer before the President continued. "Oh, fine, just fine, thank you. Look, I'm awfully sorry to bother you at that number." The receiver crackled. The President went on. "Oh, oh, yes, the Ambassador gave it to me... What's that? Oh, I get you, yes, well, maybe next time I come to Moscow."

Again the Russian Premier replied, and the President waited for him to finish. Then he said, "Yes, I'll sure look forward to that. But right now I have Ambassador De Sadeski with me, and I've brought him up to date on a certain problem which I'll describe to you in a second, but first I want him to say hello so you'll know he's here."

When he had finished speaking, the President covered the telephone with his hand and motioned to De Sadeski. He said quietly, "Tell him where you are and that you will enter into the conversation if I say anything untrue. But please don't tell him any more than that."

De Sadeski said, "Yes, but I don't have a phone."

The President waved his hand impatiently. "Give him your phone, Staines."

Staines did not appear pleased by this order. He handed his telephone stiffly to De Sadeski, who sank into Staines's chair. Staines moved away and crowded a colonel to hear on his earphone.

Ambassador De Sadeski spoke in Russian, volubly and at length. None of those around the table could understand Russian, but all of them heard several times a reference to what could have been Merkin Muffley.

The Ambassador finished his speech, waited for the reply, and then nodded grimly to the President. "I have done as you asked, but be careful, Mister President, I think he's drunk." He followed these remarks with a few choice Russian words which fortunately no one present could understand.

The President's voice when he spoke was soft and persuasive. "Hello? Yes, it's me again, Dimitri. What? Say, look, I can't hear you too well. Do you suppose they could turn that music down?" He laughed shortly. "Sure, I understand. Yes, that's much better."

A few seconds went by while he wondered exactly how to phrase his next remarks. He preceded them with a forced, nervous laugh. "Look, Dimitri, you know how we've always talked about the possibility of something going wrong with the bomb?" His cold made his pronunciation unclear and he hastily reached for a handkerchief as a query came back over the phone.

"The bomb?"

"Yes, well you know, the hydrogen bomb!... That's right. Well, apparently one of our base commanders suffered some sort of mental breakdown and ordered his planes to attack your country." He held the earphone slightly away from him as there was a series of loud noises from the other end. Admiral Randolph glanced across at General Turgidson, who raised his eyes expressively toward the ceiling.

The President said, "Well look, let me finish... let me finish... *let me finish*. That's right, a total of thirty-four planes, but they won't reach their targets for another hour." He glanced quickly at General Turgidson, who nodded. "That's right, an hour."

Again a blast of vituperation came into his ear. He said indignantly, "Well, how do you think I feel about this? Why do you think I'm calling you... no, it is not. It's most certainly not a trick. Look, I've been over all this with your Ambassador, and I repeat, it is *not a trick*.

We've been trying to recall them but there's a problem about the code... That's right, the code to recall them. You'll have to trust me on this, Dimitri, it's too complicated to explain. All right, sure I'll listen to you."

He clicked his fingers at one of the aides, who stepped forward with a cigarette and placed it between the President's lips, then held a cigarette lighter for him. The President inhaled deeply, and blew out a cloud of smoke. His hand was shaking slightly as the voice of the Premier finished.

The President said, "What are you talking about? I don't see why this thing has to mean the end of the world. Come on, don't talk like that, Dimitri. That's not very constructive."

Again Turgidson smiled his tight smile. He felt he quite liked the way the conversation was going. He glanced at the Big Board, noting how far the tracks had now encroached on Russia, and noting too the steady build-up of SAC wings heading north and the tankers heading for the refueling areas. He picked up his telephone and began to talk quietly to the SAC commander at Offutt.

The President broke in on the Premier. He said loudly, "Look, Dimitri, we're wasting time. We'd like to give your staff a complete rundown on the targets and on the flight plans and on the defense systems of the planes... that's right, if we're unable to recall the planes then I'd say we must help to destroy them, and we will do this. But who should my staff call?"

He switched his phone from right hand to left and began to write rapidly on the pad in front of him. As he wrote, he repeated the information the Russian Premier was giving him.

"The People's Central Air Defense Headquarters— that's a great name, Dimitri, where is that? Oh, in Omsk.

All right. You call them first… Uh huh…listen, do you happen to have the phone number handy? Just ask Omsk Information? Okay, Dimitri, I've got that. How long will it take for you to get back to your office?"

He waited for the reply, flicking ash from his nervously puffed cigarette on the gleaming floor of the War Room. "Well, call me as soon as you do. The number is Dudley three, three three three three extension two three six five, and listen, if you forget, just ask for the War Room, they'll be expecting your call. Okay…bye-bye."

The President covered the mouthpiece with his hand again and turned to the Ambassador. "He wants to talk to you."

Ambassador De Sadeski began to talk rapidly in Russian. Suddenly he became silent, interjecting only a few questions and finally slamming down his phone to end the conversation.

The President looked at him with apprehension. "What happened?"

De Sadeski slowly took his hand away from the telephone. Slowly he raised his head until he was looking right at the President. He said softly but bitterly, "The fools! The mad, crazy, insane fools!"

The President said quickly, "What are you talking about?"

"The Doomsday Machine."

Around the table men turned to each other, echoing De Sadeski's phrase. None of them knew what he was talking about.

"I never heard of it," Admiral Randolph said.

"Me neither," General Faceman broke in.

General Turgidson contented himself with a disgusted snort, looked at the ceiling, and said authoritatively, "There isn't such a thing."

De Sadeski ignored them. He spoke in a quiet and

metallic monotone. "The Doomsday Machine. A device which will destroy all human and animal life on earth." His control suddenly broke and he began to curse in Russian.

Though no one understood what he was saying, they realized from his way of saying it that something terrible had happened.

Doctor Strangelove realized what that something was. He began to formulate a plan to combat the disaster. He was confident that he would succeed and that his plan would be accepted when those in the room, including the President, realized the inevitable implications of what the Russian Ambassador had said.

But for the moment he was saying nothing. He wanted time to think.

LEPER COLONY

King was flying the bomber right on the deck now. He was relying on the accuracy of his radar altimeter and on the many years of experience he had behind him. He had set the radar altimeter so that it would show red when the plane's height was less than one hundred feet.

He said, "How's ole Ace, Dietrich?"

"Not in good shape."

"You got all the ECM working at maximum?"

"Maximum, King."

"Roger."

Sweets Kivel picked up his computer, adjusted the

circular scale, and wrote down some figures. Then he used the computer again and checked his results. He frowned, shook his head, and checked them again.

Lieutenant Lothar Zogg was watching this operation attentively. He said quietly to the navigator as he saw his anxious look, "Something wrong, kid?"

Sweets said, "Well, it looks rough. Hey, King, we're using an awful lot of fuel."

"Sure," King said, "this altitude we do use a lot of fuel."

Sweets shook his head again. "Yes, I know. But my calculations show we're using a lot more than we should."

King laughed. He said, "So check 'em again, Sweets. I ain't never seen a navigator yet who didn't make a mistake."

Goldberg was working busily on the CWIE, testing out the circuits. He reached to the rack above the device and pulled down a small unit to replace the unit which he thought was kaput.

The unit system was used in SAC bombers to speed repairs to damaged equipment. In the air there was no time to mend broken wires and connections. So each piece of equipment was built in a series of units which could be easily replaced.

Goldberg removed the old unit and slid the new one into place. Then he began testing again.

Dietrich bent over Ace. "Can I get you anything, Ace," he said. "Java or something?"

"Guess I'd like some water," Ace said. "Throat seems kind of dry."

Dietrich nodded his head wisely. He adopted the bed-side manner of a family physician. "Always does, this sort of case. I'll get you some water. How's the dressing?"

"It's okay," Ace said faintly.

Dietrich turned away and filled a paper cup with water.

At this height the plane was not too steady. Up-currents from the rough and rugged terrain were shaking it, and Dietrich had difficulty in taking the water to Ace without spilling it. But he succeeded, and Ace Owens sucked down with avidity the water from the cup Dietrich held for him.

He said, "That was great."

Again Dietrich nodded. "Always is," he said. "Now you try to get some sleep."

Ace closed his eyes. Dietrich watched him for a few seconds, then returned to his station.

Sweets Kivel checked his calculations for a third time and passed them across to Lothar Zogg. He said, "Lothar, you see if you can make these come out any different."

Lothar Zogg looked carefully at the figures. He reached for a computer and checked them out. After a minute he put the computer down on the table in front of them and said, "I can't see any mistakes."

Sweets said, "King, those calculations were right. I've checked them again and Lothar checked them too. We're using twice the fuel we should."

King said quickly, "But we got enough to get to the primary?"

"Sure."

"And the secondary?"

"Well yes, but…"

"But what?"

"But you know I said a few minutes ago we'd have to paddle home?"

"Awright," King said, "so we have to paddle home."

"Well now," Sweets said, "I got to amend that. Way it looks now, we'll have a long walk before we start paddling."

THE WAR ROOM—
COMMUNICATIONS CENTER

In a room behind the War Room, Air Force linguists were transmitting radio messages from staff officers to their equivalents in the Soviet Union.

They were passing details of tracks and targets and also giving information of progress of the attacking bombers.

They found that the Russian link-up was good, and the Russian officers replied to them quickly. It did not take long before both sides had established a rapport which seemed likely to end in the destruction of all the attacking bombers.

These were professionals. They were not ideologists, or people with an ax to grind, but solid, professional officers with a lifetime of experience behind them and the knowledge they were doing their job.

They talked busily as their opposite numbers in Omsk asked them for information which they freely gave on the President's instructions.

Among the items of information they supplied were these: the exact heights and speeds of the attacking bombers; their targets, primary and secondary; also details of their ECM devices and how to overcome them. Additionally they gave every detail about the bombers' fuel supply, defense systems, and the number of defense missiles carried by each bomber and how they would be employed.

They passed this information as rapidly as possible, and they noticed very quickly that the Russian staff officers were equally quick to pick up the messages and take action about them.

The American staff officers were very impressed by this. It implied that the Russian staff officers were educated.

BURPELSON AIR FORCE BASE

"They've surrendered," Ripper repeated. In his voice there were tones of both anger and hurt.

Mandrake tentatively put a hand on his elbow. He said, "They did their best, Jack. It was bound to happen. We just have to hope there weren't too many casualties."

Ripper brushed past him, still holding the heavy machine gun in his left hand. Mandrake followed him as he crossed the office. Ripper looked at his cigar, saw that it was dead, but made no attempt to relight it. He stuck it back in his mouth, then turned his head toward Mandrake, who was bending anxiously over the left arm of the chair, looking at him with great concern.

Ripper's voice was different now. It was the voice of a man who unaccountably has been let down by friends. He said, "They were my boys and they let me down. They let me down. Pretty soon those other guys are going to walk in here, you know that?"

Mandrake said lightly, "It doesn't matter, Jack. After all, we know they're on our side, you and I, Jack, don't we?"

"Are they?"

"Well of course," Mandrake said, "of course they are."

Ripper looked steadily at Mandrake, his face twitching in several places now. He said, "Group Captain, have you ever been tortured?"

"Well," Mandrake said, "yes, I have actually." Then he leaned forward and spoke urgently to Ripper. "Jack, we're getting short of time, let me know the recall code, Jack, let me have it now before it's too late."

"Who tortured you?"

"It doesn't matter," Mandrake said quickly. "Jack, just give me the recall code, we don't have much time left now."

Ripper rolled his dead cigar around his mouth. "How well did you stand up under torture, Group Captain?"

Mandrake said quietly and quickly, "Not well. No one does, you know, in the end."

"What did they get out of you?"

Mandrake laughed uneasily. "Well, nothing much actually. Don't think they really wanted anything actually. More for amusement, you might say."

Ripper looked at him intently. "Where was this?"

Mandrake said, "Well, on the railway line, you know. Building lines for bloody Japanese puff-puffs. Nasty little bastards." He paused for a moment reflectively. "Funny they can make such bloody good cameras. Jack, my dear fellow, give me the code, we don't have much time."

Ripper's cigar moved in his mouth again as he spoke. "They're going to be in here soon. I don't know how well I could stand up to torture either. They might force the code out of me."

Mandrake's laugh was nervous, almost hysterical. "No, Jack, they wouldn't do that. Anyway, we can prevent it, can't we? Just give me the code now, then everything will be all right. You'll see."

Ripper looked at him. His eyes were glazed and expressionless, almost dead. His voice was lifeless. "It can't ever be all right for me again, not after what's happened."

Mandrake said quickly, "Don't talk like that, Jack. Just give me the code, I'll pass it on, then I'll look after you. After all, these things happen, Jack. All you need is a rest. You know they'll put you in a nice hospital and these psychiatrist fellows can work wonders, and before you know it you'll be as right as rain." Urgency came into his voice. "There's very little time left. Give me the code."

Ripper mumbled, "It won't matter about the code, they won't take any notice of that. They'll be in here soon and they'll get me."

Mandrake's voice was artificially bright and lively. "Not a chance, Jack. You just leave it to me. And if they do try it, we'll fight them off, just like we did before. You and me, Jack, eh? You hold the machine gun and I'll feed you, just like we did before! Jack, please give me the code."

Ripper said, "'Joe for King,' Group Captain, that's what they had written on the walls. Well, I tell you something, Joe ain't ever going to be king. Joe's dead, Group Captain, and if he wasn't, he soon would be."

Ripper stood and Mandrake stood also. Ripper began to walk slowly across the office, the empty bullet cases clinking as his dragging feet moved through them. He was trailing the machine gun in his left hand.

As he was passing the desk, the machine gun dropped from his hand and crashed to the floor. Mandrake hastened to pick it up and said, "Jack, your machine gun, don't you want it, Jack?"

Ripper slowly and deliberately took off his uniform jacket. Mandrake leaned the machine gun against a chair and said, "Here, let me have your coat, Jack. I'll hold it for you."

Ripper handed over the coat without a word and turned away, moving like an automaton toward the door of his office.

Mandrake followed him, the General's coat folded across his arm. At the door Ripper paused. He turned and said, "I'm going for a walk, Group Captain. I don't know how I could stand up. Remember the purity of your bodily essences, and remember 'Joe for King,' Group Captain. Remember the significance of 'Joe for King.'" Then he went through the door, slamming it behind him.

For a moment Mandrake was too paralyzed to move. Then he went quickly to the door and ran out into the corridor. There was no sign of Ripper anywhere. Mandrake searched for him for several minutes but in vain. Then he returned dejectedly to the office.

THE WAR ROOM

In the War Room there was silence except for the clicking of electronic devices as the displays on the Big Board changed, and telephones were replaced as everyone pondered the implication of what the Russian Ambassador had said. Everyone looked toward him.

De Sadeski said slowly and with dignity, "A Doomsday Machine, gentlemen. That's what I said and that's what I meant. When it is detonated it will produce enough lethal radioactive fallout so within twelve months the surface of the earth will be as dead as the moon."

General Turgidson said loudly, "That's ridiculous, De Sadeski. Our studies show the worst fallout is down to a tolerably safe level after two weeks."

De Sadeski smiled coldly. "Have you ever heard of Cobalt-Thorium-G?"

"What about it?"

"It has," De Sadeski said, "a radioactive half-life of ninety-three years."

Around the table there was a buzz of talk and everyone instinctively looked at the senior aide who represented the Atomic Energy Commission. He nodded grimly.

De Sadeski continued. "If you take, say, fifty H-bombs in the hundred-megaton range and jacket them with Cobalt-Thorium-G, when they are exploded they will produce a Doomsday shroud, a lethal cloud of radioactivity which will encircle the earth for ninety-three years."

The President ignored the murmurs round the table. He spoke directly to De Sadeski. "Mister Ambassador, I'm afraid I don't understand something. Is the Premier threatening to explode this if our planes carry through their attack?"

De Sadeski said emphatically, "No, sir. It is not a thing a sane man would do. The Doomsday Machine is designed to trigger itself *automatically!*"

"But then, surely he can disarm it somehow."

"No! It is designed to explode if any attempt is ever made to untrigger it!"

General Turgidson snorted. He turned to the colonel beside him and said softly, "It's an obvious commie trick." He jerked his head toward the President and there was bitterness in his voice. "And he sits there wasting precious time."

President Muffley was bewildered. He could not grasp the implications of what De Sadeski had said. He thought for a moment, began to speak, hesitated, and lapsed into thought again. De Sadeski looked at him impassively. Finally the President said, "But surely,

Ambassador, this is absolute madness. Why should you build such a thing?"

De Sadeski shrugged his shoulders expressively. "There were those of us who fought against it, but in the end we could not keep up in the Peace Race, the Space Race and the Arms Race. Our deterrent began to lack credibility. Our people grumbled for more nylons and lipsticks. Our Doomsday project cost us just a fraction of what we had been spending in just a single year. But the deciding factor was when we learned your country was working along similar lines, and we were afraid of a Doomsday Gap."

"That's preposterous. I've never approved anything like that!"

"Our source was the New York *Times*."

President Muffley turned to his Director of Weapons Research and Development. "Doctor Strangelove, do we have anything like this in the works?"

Doctor Strangelove spoke with Germanic precision. He emphasized his point with abrupt movements of his right hand. "Mister President, under the authority granted me as Director of Weapons Research and Development, I commissioned a study of this project by the Bland Corporation last year. Based on the findings of the report, my conclusion was that this idea was not a practical deterrent for reasons which at this moment must be all too obvious."

President Muffley passed a weary hand across his head. "You mean it's unquestionably possible for them to have built this thing? Absolutely unquestionably possible?"

The Russian Ambassador broke in. "Mister President, the technique required is easily within the reach of even the smallest nuclear power. It requires only the *will* to do so."

"But," Muffley said, "is it really possible for it to be triggered automatically and at the same time impossible to untrigger?"

Before the Russian Ambassador could reply, Doctor Strangelove said quickly, "But precisely. Mister President, it is not only possible, it is essential. That is the whole idea of this machine. Deterrence is the art of producing in the mind of the enemy the fear to attack. And so because of the automated and irrevocable decision-making process which rules out human meddling, the Doomsday Machine is terrifying, simple to understand, and completely credible and convincing."

On the other side of the table General Turgidson turned again to the colonel beside him. He said, "What kind of a name is that—Strangelove? That ain't no Kraut name."

The colonel whispered back to him, "Changed it when he became a U.S. citizen. Used to be Merkwürdigichliebe."

Turgidson chuckled unpleasantly. "Well," he said, "a Kraut by any other name, eh, Bill?"

President Muffley said, "But this is fantastic, Doctor Strangelove. How can it be triggered automatically?"

Strangelove said, "Sir, it is remarkably simple to do that. When you merely wish to bury bombs there is no limit to the size. I should say rather that they are not bombs, merely devices. After they are buried they are connected to a gigantic complex of computers. A specific and closely defined set of circumstances under which the bombs are to be exploded is programed into the tape memory banks. A single roll of tape can store all the information, say, in a twenty-five volume encyclopedia, *and* analyze it for any desired piece of information in fifteen seconds. In order for the memory banks to decide when such a triggering circumstance has occurred, they are linked to a vast interlocking network of data-input sensors which are stationed throughout the country and orbited in satellites. These sensors monitor heat, ground shock, sound, atmospheric pressure and radioactivity."

Strangelove turned so he looked directly at De Sadeski. "There is only one thing I don't understand, Mister Ambassador. The whole point of the Doomsday Machine is lost if you keep it a secret. Why didn't you tell the world?"

De Sadeski turned away. He said quietly but distinctly, "It was to be announced at the Party Congress on Monday. As you know, the Premier loves surprises."

President Muffley said, "Ambassador, I assume then if the attack is carried through by our planes, this thing will be set off?"

The Russian Ambassador spoke loudly and convincingly. He appeared reluctant, but it was his duty to say it, and he said it. "Yes, Mister President, it will. Though I don't think..."

General Faceman, the Army Chief of Staff, took a message from an aide who had entered the room, scanned it quickly, then interrupted the Ambassador. "Excuse me, sir. I think we're beginning to pick up some yardage. The base at Burpelson has just surrendered."

The President swallowed hard. This might just be it. This could be the break he had been looking for. He said, "Have you got the commanding general on the phone?"

General Faceman was confident. He could not resist looking across at Turgidson who had told him earlier that the base could be defended indefinitely. Turgidson looked away. Faceman said, "We will in a minute, sir. Look, Mister President, I just hate to say this but if you're unable to convince the general..."

He looked down for a moment and crushed a cigarette in the ashtray in front of him. Then he spoke firmly. "If you're unable to convince the general, will you please let me have a few words with my boys down there? I hate to suggest this, but they might be able to sort of, well, you know, convince him to give us the code."

BURPELSON AIR FORCE BASE

Group Captain Mandrake stood motionless beside Ripper's desk. His expression was fixed, and he was staring with dull, shocked eyes at a wallet of photographs. He had seen Ripper looking at this wallet before, but this was the first time he had seen the photographs. They were of Ripper's mother and father.

He shuffled absently through the clutter of objects on Ripper's desk, and suddenly his attention was drawn to a ruled yellow legal-size tablet, on which he had seen Ripper doodling. He picked it up and looked at it closely. On it, scribbled in bold letters, was the phrase "Purity of Essence." Around it were drawn weird birds, diamond shapes and triangles, rifles, and the number seven. There was also the phrase "Joe for King" repeated six or seven times.

Mandrake studied in particular the phrases which Ripper had written. An idea was beginning to form in his mind.

He was so absorbed in his speculation that he did not notice the entrance of a crew-cut Army officer. This was

Colonel "Bat" Guano, the commander of the battalion which had assaulted Burpelson.

Guano crept into the room cautiously with his carbine held forward ready to fire.

Mandrake was muttering to himself, "Joe for King. I wonder. JFK...FJK...KFJ."

Guano peered at him suspiciously. He said in a tight, tough voice, "Okay, soldier, just what the hell is going on here? What kind of uniform is that? Get your hands on your head."

Mandrake looked at him absently, and then looked away again. He kept on muttering, "JFK...KFJ...FJK" until Colonel Guano ripped off two shots which tore into the desk. Guano had much experience of combat and found this to be a most effective way of convincing a prisoner he was just that. Mandrake, shocked by the near impact of the shots, hastily raised his hands.

Guano said, "Quickly! Quickly! Hands on head, soldier. What kind of uniform is that, soldier?"

"I happen to be Group Captain Lionel Mandrake of the Royal Air Force, General Ripper's executive officer."

"*Keep 'em up! Keep 'em up!* Where's General Ripper?"

Mandrake motioned with his head. "Well, I'm afraid General Ripper's disappeared, actually." He laughed nervously. "Pity you missed him, actually. He just sort of ran out."

Guano turned and moved across to the open door of the office. But as he moved he kept the muzzle of his carbine pointing at Mandrake, who turned to watch him. Guano looked down the empty corridor then swung back to Mandrake. "So he just ran out, just like that, huh?"

"That's right," Mandrake said quickly. "Now look, Colonel, can we stop playing..."

"You think we were playing games out there?"

Guano's voice was flat and unemotional, the voice of a professional accustomed to the unpleasant sights of combat and violent death. He looked at Mandrake with suspicion.

Mandrake said, "Please, Colonel, I've got a terrific hunch on the recall code, you know. I think I know what it is and I simply must get in touch with Strategic Air Command Headquarters." He began to move toward the phone.

Guano said menacingly, "Just keep them up nice on your head, Group Captain whatever-your-name-is. Do you have any witness to this thing?"

Mandrake swallowed. He tried desperately to put into his voice a calmness which would convince this soldier. He said, "Now look here, Colonel, you've got this thing all confused in your mind somehow. But there's not a second to lose. You see, I think it's a variation of 'Joe for King.' It was a kind of recurrent theme. It could be some variation…JFK…FJK…KJF…KFJ." His voice died away as Guano pushed the carbine forward at him.

Guano was becoming convinced now that he was facing a lunatic. Besides, he was suspicious of Mandrake's strange uniform and long hair. Perverts let their hair grow long, he knew. They liked to dress up in fancy clothes, too. He said soothingly, "Sure, fella, sure. Now just keep your hands nice and neat on the top of your head, and let's start walking out of here. Okay, pal?"

Mandrake said quickly, "Colonel, don't you know what's happened?"

"Now just calm down like I said, fella, and start walking."

"Well then, I mean I suppose you're not fully in the picture then, are you, Colonel? Don't you know that General Ripper went mad as a bloody March hare? He sent the entire bloody wing to attack the Soviets!"

Guano looked thoughtfully at Mandrake. There had to be some reason, he knew, for the assault being ordered on the base, but he shrugged it off. He said, "Now look, don't get excited, fella."

Mandrake said desperately, "Colonel, if we don't get cracking on this, the whole world may go for a Burton."

Guano stepped back a pace. Mandrake looked at him carefully. He thought he could detect an expression of doubt on Guano's face. He pressed the advantage, speaking fast and distinctly. "Now look, just let me pick up this nice red telephone that connects to SAC headquarters. See."

He moved forward to the phone and, as if he were talking to a child, said, "Now, you see, I'm picking up the phone nice and slow, right? Hello? Hello?… Damn, must be dead. I guess the lines were hit during the fighting."

Colonel Guano was watching him like a hawk.

Mandrake said, "Now see, I'm picking up this ordinary telephone." He lifted the other telephone on the desk and held it to his ear. Then he saw that the line had been cut by a shot and the telephone was not connected. "It's no use, this is something must have happened during that idiotic fighting." He slammed the receiver back on its rest.

Guano said quietly, "Now listen to me, you fruit cake. I've got wounded men outside and you've wasted enough of my time."

Mandrake was certain he knew the code. He lost his temper and shouted at Guano, "Damn it, you blasted American idiot! Can't you get it through that thick G.I. brain of yours that we're on to something infernally important here?"

Colonel Guano stepped back a pace. Again he ripped a shot into the top of the desk. After the echo of the shot died away he said, "Now, snap out of it, fella, you hear me?"

Mandrake by this time was beyond shock. He said, "What the *hell* do you think you're doing?"

"Start walking."

Mandrake shrugged. He walked across the office, his hands on his head. Guano walked behind him, the carbine pointed at Mandrake's back.

Mandrake half turned. He said, "Colonel, while there's still time, I must ask you, just *what is it* you think has been going on here this morning?"

Guano said coldly, "If you want to know what I think, I think you're some kind of deviated pervert. I think General Ripper discovered your perversion, and that you engineered a mutiny of perverts. On top of that my orders didn't say nothing about planes attacking Russia. All I was told was to put General Ripper on the phone with the President of the United States."

Mandrake swung around completely. "Hold on, that's it, the President!"

"What about the President?"

Mandrake's voice was excited now. "You said the President wants to speak to General Ripper, didn't you? Well, Ripper's not here, is he? And I'm his executive officer, so he'll bloody well want to speak to me, don't you see?" He pointed to the pay phone near them. "And there's a phone booth there, and that line's sure to be open."

Guano looked at Mandrake incredulously. He said, "You want to talk to the President of the United States? You?"

Mandrake's voice was quiet, but completely convincing. "Colonel, unless you stop this silly-ass nonsense and let me use that phone, I can damned well assure you the Court of Inquiry on this will give you such a pranging, you'll count yourself lucky to wear the uniform of a toilet attendant."

Guano swung his carbine from one hand to the other. He looked first at Mandrake, then at the pay phone, then back to Mandrake again. He said slowly and reluctantly, "Okay, you see if you can get the President of the United States on the telephone. But if you try any perversions in there, I'll blow your head off!"

Without replying, Mandrake dashed into the phone booth. He fumbled in his pocket, found a dime and dialed the operator, then waited for the operator's voice.

When it came, he immediately began to talk. "Hello, operator? This is Group Captain Mandrake at Burpelson Air Force Base. Something rather important has come up, and I would like to place an emergency person-to-person call to President Merkin Muffley in the Pentagon, Washington, D.C. No, I'm perfectly serious… that's right…that's right, the President, President of the United States." He paused. "How much? Two dollars and seventy-five cents. Just a moment."

He quickly counted his change and saw that it was not enough, then beat his pockets looking for more. But he had no more change.

Outside, Guano looked at him suspiciously. He held his carbine so it was lined up on Mandrake's head.

Mandrake spoke frantically into the phone. "Can you make this a collect call, operator?… That's right, Group Captain Lionel Mandrake, Burpelson Air Force Base. What? Well, look here, tell them it's terrifically important, will you?" He paused again. "All right, just a moment… "

He continued to hold the receiver in his right hand and pushed open the door with his left. He said, "Colonel, they aren't allowed to accept any long-distance collect calls at the Pentagon. Look here, I need fifty-five cents."

Bat Guano said contemptuously, "I wouldn't carry loose change going into combat, fruit cake."

Mandrake spoke into the phone again. "Operator, how much would a call be station-to-station? Oh, I'd still be minus twenty cents. You couldn't put it through, could you? It's terrifically important."

He listened to the reply, then said, "All right, just a second, operator, I'll try to get it." He covered the mouthpiece and turned toward Guano. Over the colonel's shoulder he saw a Coke machine he had often used in the past. Suddenly there was hope. He said, "Colonel, I want you to shoot the lock off that Coke machine. There's bound to be a lot of change in there."

Colonel Guano was unimpressed. "That's private property, Group Captain."

Mandrake said emphatically, "Colonel, just imagine what's going to happen to your career, when the Court of Inquiry learns that you have so completely obstructed this call to the President." He spoke again to the operator. "Just a moment, operator, I know I have the change somewhere."

Guano sensed the urgency in Mandrake's voice. What the hell, he thought, there'd been a lot of shots round the place anyway. And maybe this guy might have something important. He turned and carefully, almost apologetically, fired two shots into the coin box of the Coke machine.

A profusion of coins spilled on the floor.

And a stream of Coca-Cola splashed into the colonel's face.

Mandrake scrabbled on the floor and came up with a fistful of coins.

Guano said, "You got a handkerchief?"

"Don't you have one?" Mandrake said coldly.

"I wouldn't carry handkerchiefs going into combat, either," Guano said.

"No time now." Mandrake rushed into the phone booth and picked up the receiver.

"Operator…operator…operator, where the hell are you, operator?"

"Well I mean, this is terribly important, you know. No, I *didn't* use bad language… Well, how can I tell what you mean by bad language. Now please, I beg you, put this call through. I have the change right here."

Mandrake slid coins into the slot and waited impatiently for the call to come through.

He heard the clicking of distant connections, then a female voice said, "Dudley three, three three three three."

Mandrake said quickly, "I have to talk to the President. An urgent message. Will you connect me fast, please?"

The voice said, "Who is this?"

"It's Grou…never mind that, it's Burpelson Air Force Base. You'll find he wants to talk to us… All right, I'll hold on. But please make it as fast as you can.

Guano had brushed away most of the liquid from his face and wiped his hands on his stained uniform. He poked his head into the door of the phone booth and said suspiciously, "What's going on?"

Mandrake said, "I'm through to the Pentagon. They're trying to contact the President."

Guano moved away and leaned against the wall opposite the phone booth. He watched Mandrake with continued suspicion.

Mandrake heard a click at the other end of the line as a phone was lifted. He said, "Look here, this is Burpelson Air Force Base. Is this the President?" He added as an afterthought, "Sir."

A deep voice said, "No, it is not. Is this Burpelson?"

Mandrake said, "Yes, this is Burpelson, but I want the President."

"You can pass your message to me."

"How do I know that?"

"Because I tell you, Burpelson. For your information I am General Faceman's aide. The President is busy on another line."

Mandrake thought for a moment. He looked at his watch and saw that the bombers must now be close to their targets. "All right, but please remember this is jolly important, I mean the message must be passed on immediately, or we'll all be in big trouble."

"It'll be passed on."

Mandrake said, "Well here it is. You know poor General Ripper went completely bloody mad and sent a wing against the Soviets?"

"We do."

"Well you see, I think it's 'Joe for King.'"

The voice at the other end said, "What was that again? This must be a bad line. I thought you said something like 'Joe King.'"

"No, no, no," Mandrake said desperately. "Well never mind, but I think you'll find the recall code is some combination of the letters JFK plus whatever number fluorine is in the periodic table... No, I *don't* know the number, but you must have some people in the Pentagon who know it."

The voice said, "Now, let me get this straight. You think the recall code is a combination of the letters JFK plus the number of chlorine?"

"No," Mandrake shouted in exasperation, "fluorine!"

"Fluorine?"

"Yes," Mandrake shouted, "fluorine. F-L-U-O-R-I-N-E, fluorine."

"And you believe that's it?"

Mandrake said firmly, "I do."

"Okay, I'll pass it on."

Mandrake heard a click as the line went dead. He replaced the phone and came out of the booth.

Guano looked at him with slightly less suspicion than previously. He said, "Did you get him? Did you speak with the President?"

"No," Mandrake said, "I spoke with the aide of a General Faceman. He is passing the information on."

"Okay," Guano said. "Well, maybe I was wrong about you, but let's not try any tricks, huh? Let's you and I go out and try to locate General Ripper."

Mandrake smoothed his hair abstractedly. He realized suddenly that he was improperly dressed. He said, "Look here, Colonel, I just want to go back to my office for a moment and locate my headgear. Can't be seen walking around without correct headgear."

Guano said, "Well okay, but let's make it fast. We gotta locate the General."

They walked quickly to Mandrake's office. Mandrake collected his uniform cap and put it on. The telephone rang. Mandrake picked it up and said, "Yes, this is the executive. In what?... Five minutes ago. I see." He put the phone down and turned to Guano. "I don't think it'll be much use looking for General Ripper, Colonel."

Guano immediately became suspicious again. "Why in hell not?"

"Because," Mandrake said slowly, "he just took off in his personal plane. And not only is he mad, but he's drunk as a bloody skunk!"

LEPER COLONY

Lieutenant Goldberg finished his checks on the CWIE. He said, "King, I've tried to unravel it but it's hopeless. All the radio gear is kaput, like I said, and I just can't repair it."

He looked down at the CWIE, which could be seen to be hopelessly smashed and twisted, now he had taken the front off it.

King said, "What happened, Goldy?"

Goldberg looked at the gear and shook his head. "Maybe," he said, "the emergency self-destruct mechanism got hit and blew itself up."

King said, "Well, awright, don't let's worry too much about that now. Lothar, how about them firecrackers?"

Lothar Zogg looked quickly at his circuit lights. "Everything seems to check out okay."

"Sweets?"

"Okay, King."

"Dietrich, ECM?"

Dietrich looked closely at his equipment. He said slowly, "King, ECM's okay."

"Awright, keep it blastin'. You figure it's upset their radar?"

Dietrich said, "Ain't much radar can reach us down here, King, but what there is we'll sure as hell upset it."

King said, "Okay, keep it goin'. Goldy, you mean all our radio gear is out?"

Lieutenant Goldberg said positively, "It's out. The CWIE I just can't repair."

"So repair somethin' else."

Goldberg said patiently, "Look, King, when we're flying on a mission like this, it don't make no difference. Maybe the other radios are okay, but they're no good to use if the CWIE is wrecked. We just can't receive any messages."

"You sure?"

"I'm sure."

"Can we transmit?"

Goldberg said, "Well maybe. I just don't know."

"Okay," King said, "forget it, Goldy. I guess from here on in we ain't gonna want any more information. What the hell could those guys tell us anyway?"

"Well," Sweets Kivel said, "maybe they could tell us the war's over."

Lothar Zogg said, "Are you kidding?"

"Yeah," Kivel agreed, "just kidding."

King peered forward at the difficult terrain he would have to cross. He was an expert, a good pilot who could see his way when everyone else turned back. He could feel he was going to get to the target and deliver his load. He hunched forward and concentrated as the snowy terrain flashed past under the bomber.

THE WAR ROOM

In the War Room everyone sitting around the great table was concentrating his attention on the large display map of Russia. As they watched, the arrow-like track indicating the dead reckoning position of each aircraft suddenly began to look off and change direction.

In the room there was a background of short-wave transmissions, which some enthusiast had switched through to let everyone hear the airplanes acknowledging the recall code. Around the table there was a general cheer, such as one might hear at an election victory, backslapping by people sitting next to each other, and great high spirits.

A sample radio message went like this: ROGER, SEVEN-TWO ZEBRA ABLE, CONFIRMING, ACKNOWLEDGE AND CONFIRM MISSION CANCELED, RETURNING TO BASE.

The President put his inhaler to his face, quickly pulled it away, and looked across the table at General Faceman. "What was the name of the officer who called me from Burpelson?"

Faceman said, "I didn't speak to him, sir. But Colonel Guano was commanding the airborne battalion. I imagine *he* made the call."

"I want that officer upped to brigadier general and flown to Washington. I want to decorate him personally."

"Yes, sir."

The President turned to Turgidson. "Let me know when all the recalls are acknowledged."

"They're almost all in now," Turgidson said quickly.

"They are?" The President looked at the Big Board. "How many planes did we lose?"

Turgidson himself looked at the Big Board. He moistened his lips with his tongue. "We're not certain, sir. You see, the Big Board is only a dead-reckoning indicator. It plots the courses the planes would normally be on. It does show four splashed, but that is based entirely on enemy reports."

"I see."

General Turgidson suddenly climbed on a chair and asked for silence. As the Big Board continued to show the bombers turning and heading back from their targets, he said, "Gentlemen, gentlemen."

All gave their attention to him. The room was very quiet.

Turgidson said piously, "Gentlemen, I'm not a sentimentalist by nature, but I wonder now if I don't know what's in every heart in this room." He paused, then continued. "Gentlemen, I want to suggest that we get down on our knees and say a short prayer of thanks for our deliverance."

The President inclined his head gravely, pushed back his chair, and slowly sank to his knees. Soon all were kneeling except De Sadeski and Doctor Strangelove. But Strangelove made the gesture of leaning forward, while at the same time appearing to have some difficulty in controlling a tendency of his right arm to jerk upwards.

De Sadeski looked round the room. He said with some scorn, "Excuse me, but I'm afraid I have far more urgent matters to attend to."

There were angry and astonished murmurs from the group.

De Sadeski ignored them and continued. "But before I leave, I wish to state unequivocally that my Government will not be satisfied with a polite note of regret over this shocking aggression against the peace-loving people of the Soviet Union."

The President rose slowly to his feet. He inhaled thoughtfully on his inhaler while he glared at De Sadeski.

Around the room comments were heard.

"Well, that cuts it," from Turgidson.

"That commie punk," from Randolph.

President Muffley slowly raised his hands for silence. The buzz of comment died away.

The President said, "Damn you, De Sadeski! Damn you! This was the result of one man's action, a mentally unbalanced person, and we have no monopoly on lunatics."

Ambassador De Sadeski's heavy face was sneering. He said, "It is very convenient for you to place the blame on someone not present to answer."

"How dare you address me in such a manner!" The President was really angry now, working himself up into a rage, which those who had seen him in conference with political leaders in the past knew would be violent.

De Sadeski said coldly, "Please don't shout, Mister President."

The President said, "I have warned about this danger for years. During those futile disarmament conferences at Geneva I have stuck my neck out time and time again."

De Sadeski said contemptuously, "Bah! You've never wanted disarmament. It would wreck your economy."

"That's nonsense! We could spend exactly the same amount on schools, highways, and space."

De Sadeski also was now becoming bitter and angry. "All you ever wanted to do was spy in our country."

President Muffley was becoming angrier. "You know that is a lie, De Sadeski. You could not expect us to destroy *our* weapons without having the faintest idea of what you were doing inside your country!"

"And you, Mister President, could not expect us to let you spy in our country before you destroyed your weapons."

The President said nothing for several seconds. His face became whiter and in his temple a small vein was beating heavily. And then he exploded. "Now listen to me, De Sadeski! Despite total mistrust and mutual suspicion, we both place an incredible trust in each other; a trust far greater than disarmament and inspection would ever require. We trust each other to maintain the balance of terror, to behave rationally and to do nothing which would cause a war by accident or miscalculation or madness. Now *this* is a ridiculous trust, because even assuming we both had perfect intentions, we cannot honestly guarantee anything. There are too many fingers on the buttons. There are too many reasons both mechanical and human for the system to fail. What a marvelous thing for the fate of the world to depend on—a state of mind, a mood, a feeling, a moment of anger, an impulse, ten minutes of poor judgment, a sleepless night."

The President took his handkerchief again and blew his nose loudly. A little color was back in his face, but he still glared at De Sadeski.

He continued in a quieter voice. "And so what is the hope? The behavior of nations has always been despicable. The great nations have always acted like gangsters, and the small nations like prostitutes. They have bribed and threatened and murdered their way through history. And now the Bomb has become an even greater enemy to every nation than they ever have been, or ever could be, to each other. Even disarmament is not enough. We can never entirely get rid of the Bomb because the knowledge of how to make it will always now be with us. Unless we learn to create a new system of law and morality between nations, then we will surely exterminate ourselves, just as we almost did today."

De Sadeski remained impassive. He was about to speak, when Staines plucked urgently at the President's sleeve. He said, "Mister President, Soviet Premier Kissof is calling again. He is back in his office."

The President looked again at De Sadeski, then reached forward and picked up the phone.

LEPER COLONY

Leper Colony was only a few feet above the ground. King smiled. This was flying. He looked ahead and saw he would have to turn in to a valley between two big rises.

He said, "Sweets, terrain ahead looks pretty rough."

Sweets said, "Gets easier later, King."

"Okay." King expertly piloted the bomber through the valley. This was *real* flying.

Sweets said, "King, we're still using too much fuel down here. It's gonna be a long walk after we hit the primary target."

Lieutenant Goldberg said, "Okay, so we walk."

Dietrich said, "I can walk." He moved forward to look at Ace Owens.

Lothar Zogg said, "Well, a walk is a walk is a walk."

Dietrich bent over Ace. He had already administered an injection of morphine, from the package in the airplane, to the wounded copilot.

He returned to his position and said, "King, Ace is sleeping."

"Well, that's good."

"Yeah, but his breathing is kind of light."'

King frowned. "That's bad."

"That's bad," Dietrich repeated.

Lieutenant Goldberg said, "King, the CWIE is definitely right out. There ain't nothing I can do to make it work, and that's all there is to it."

King said equably, "Okay, Goldy, so fergit about it."

Goldberg said, "Forget about it?"

"Sure, fergit about it. What you think they want to talk to us now fer?"

Sweets Kivel finished some calculations. He said,

"King, that fuel consumption is still working out pretty bad."

"Roger," King said.

"Can't we go higher?"

King looked out at the terrain ahead of them. He thought about Sweets's query.

He banked the plane expertly to port to evade a long slope which was tilting up toward them.

After he straightened out he said, "Listen, Sweets, this is the deal. With the ECM workin' an' us stayin' on the deck, I don't figure they kin track us with radar, an' we oughta be able to make it to the primary target. Now I know we're burnin' a lotta juice down here an' we may not have enough left to git us back to a usable base. The way I see it, after we hit the primary we'll head fer the coast an' then bail out when she drinks it all."

"Well," Sweets said, "if it's okay with you, King, I guess it's okay with me."

Dietrich, who had been watching his radarscope closely, put a transparent overlay on the surface of the tube and checked his chronometer. The movement of three blips had appeared against the range scale marked on the overlay. Then he noticed a fourth blip appear.

He said urgently, "King, I've got four blips. They must be fighters."

"Are they on an intercept course?"

"Right on the button, King. And they got a lot of closing speed, on a dead intercept course."

"They must have got lucky and made a visual contact."

Dietrich said, "They're fighters all right. Closing speed about Mach one-eight. Range thirty miles. Altitude fifteen thousand."

"Four, you say?"

"That's right, four."

"How kin they see us from up there?" King said musingly. "We're close enough to the ground so the radar returns would get mixed up in the ground returns. Like I said, they must have got lucky and made a visual contact. You're sure they're on to us?"

Dietrich made another mark on the overlay and said, "I'm sure, all right. They're losing height, down to eleven thousand now, steady on an intercept course."

Lieutenant Goldberg said quickly, "Could be they've got a heat-seeking guidance system as well as radar. We had a lecture about it last month from the A-Two boys."

"Yeah, could be," King said. "What range now, Dietrich?"

"Range twenty miles."

"Prepare to fire missiles."

"How many, King?"

"Many as you think you need."

"Okay," Dietrich said, "preparing missiles one through eight. That leaves four to use if another fighter gets to us before we reach the primary."

"Roger, one through eight," King said.

Firing the missiles was a task for a team which consisted of Goldberg and Dietrich. Dietrich was primarily responsible, since he controlled the detection radar. But Goldberg had the responsibility for seeing that the air-to-air missiles were primed and ready to go.

Dietrich said, "Okay, make one through eight ready."

Goldberg rapidly flipped the switches in front of him. He said, "One through eight ready."

Dietrich placed his overlay on the tube of his radarscope, watched while the blips slid down the etched line on the transparency, and said, "Fire missile salvo one through eight."

Lieutenant Goldberg pressed the button.

The rockets slid from the tail of the bomber. Above

them two black radar blisters gave the initial guidance they needed to direct them toward the fighters. As soon as they had locked on to the target they would need no more guidance. Their detection system was sensitive enough so they could home on the attacking fighter without more guidance from the bomber. They had to have the path shown to them, but they did not need to be taught how to walk it.

Dietrich said, "Missiles fired!"

"Roger."

Dietrich and Goldberg watched the scopes as the traces moved out toward the attacking fighters.

The traces, after moving fast across the screens, merged in with the fighter blips. When they touched, the fighter blips flared up brightly for a second on the screens, then disappeared.

Dietrich said, "Got 'em!"

Goldberg said, "Got 'em *all*!"

And suddenly another explosion rocked *Leper Colony*.

A small fire broke out in the rear of the bombing-navigation section. Lothar Zogg pushed a button and grabbed an extinguisher.

The flight deck filled with smoke again, but it dispersed very quickly, drawn off through the holes in the side of the airplane.

King said, "What the hell was that?"

Lieutenant Goldberg said, "I think one of those fighters must have gotten something off before they were hit."

"How's Ace?"

"Still out," Dietrich said.

King had held back on the controls while the smoke obscured his vision. Now as it cleared he took *Leper Colony* down to the deck again.

He said, "Check on damage."

Lothar Zogg said, "We got another hole in the starboard side low down."

"Equipment?"

"Seems okay."

"Mine's okay," Sweets Kivel said.

"Joe?"

"No more than already, King. The CWIE is still out, but Dietrich's equipment looks good."

"Where the hell is Dietrich?" King said. There was a trace of irritation in his voice.

Dietrich responded immediately. "Why, King, I'm right here with old Ace. See, Goldy's watching the ECM and I thought I'd better administer to Ace."

"Well awright," King said, slightly mollified. "I wouldn't want you to neglect ole Ace."

"I'm *not* neglecting him."

Sweets Kivel broke in on them. "King, you noticed our fuel state?"

King looked at the fuel gauges. It was impossible, he thought, but there it was. He said, "We must of been hit in the starboard tanks, huh, Sweets?"

The navigator said, "That's what it looks to me, King. Maybe the tanks, maybe a transfer line. I don't know what the answer is now."

King looked at the ancestral portraits. "Neither do I," he said, "but I'll sure as hell figure it out."

Dietrich suddenly said, "King, Ace is dead."

"What the hell you mean he's dead?"

Dietrich's voice was quiet. "He's dead, King, that's all there is."

King said, "Hell. He was a good guy, Ace, but that's war, men."

Lieutenant Goldberg assisted Lieutenant Dietrich to close Ace Owens's eyes and cover him with a blanket. "Yes," he said, "that's war."

THE WAR ROOM

Everyone seated round the great table listened attentively as President Muffley spoke to the Russian Premier.

He said, "Hello? Premier Kissof? That's right, it's Merkin." He frowned. "Oh no, there must be some mistake. Uh-huh, yes I did get you, but just a second." He looked toward General Turgidson. "The Russian Premier claims one plane is still attacking, and his staff believe its target might be Laputa."

General Turgidson smiled. "Well now, that's impossible, Mister President. Look at the Big Board. Thirty-four planes attacking, thirty recalls acknowledged, four splashed, and one of those four was targeted for Laputa."

President Muffley said into his phone, "Hello, Dimitri? Yes, well look, we got an acknowledgment from every plane except the four you shot down…what do you mean three?…You mean it's only damaged and still coming in? …I see, wait just a second will you?" He looked again at Turgidson.

There was a hum of talk round the table as the men there discussed this news.

But Turgidson was unaffected. He was studying the Big Board. In his opinion the threat to America was increasing significantly. He ignored the President's conversation about the fourth bomber which might be damaged but still flying and said, "Mister President, I should like to call your attention to the five hundred-plus enemy planes building up over the Arctic."

The President swung round in his chair and gave his full attention to the Big Board. As he turned, several of the displays changed, and both a bigger bomber threat and more submarines were shown on all sides of the

North American continent.

General Turgidson said loudly, "Mister President, I'm beginning to smell a big, fat, commie rat. Suppose Kissof is lying about that fourth plane, just looking for an excuse to clobber us. If the spaghetti hits the fan now, we're really in trouble."

The President distractedly shrugged away Turgidson's remark as he watched the display map of Russia. The thirty-four tracks which were previously displayed had been removed. But one track continued on toward its primary and secondary targets.

The President talked into his telephone again. "Hello?...Say, look, Dimitri, if this report is true, and if by some extremely unlikely possibility you are unable to destroy the plane before it bombs its target, I assume that such an isolated nuclear incident would not trigger off the Doomsday Machine?...It depends on the total megatonnage exploded? Well, the plane carries two 20-megaton bombs—how does that sound? What do you mean you're not sure? General—who isn't there? Well, somebody else must know. You're checking? All right, I'll hold."

He looked again at the track approaching its target, then said in response to sound from the receiver, "What? What are we going to do if it doesn't go off? Well, I should think we'd all breathe a profound sigh of relief ...Oh, you mean what are we going to do about the damage? Well, naturally, we are prepared to pay full compensation. At least we're lucky it's just an isolated missile base, and that there aren't a lot of people involved. I'd hate to have to equate human lives in dollars and cents... What? Where is it? Two miles from *where*?... No, I didn't know. Our map shows only military targets. How many people? Two million seven hundred and twenty-nine thousand?"

General Turgidson whispered suspiciously to the colonel at his side, "Have we got that place down as a two-point-seven-two megadeaths situation?"

The President glanced at the North American threat display screen. It showed an increase in Russian build-up. He reached for his telephone again. "I must have your assurance that your government will not treat this as a hostile act. Well of course it's not a friendly act, but I mean to say, this should not be treated as an act of war. Uh huh... What... *What*? Come on now, Dimitri, that's a pretty inhuman sort of idea, isn't it? Do you mean to say you actually expect us to let you take out Detroit? You must be out of your mind. You can't just trade people like pieces on a chess board."

General Turgidson, who had moved behind the President during the conversation, shoved in front of him a loose leaf book entitled "World Targets in Megadeaths." He pointed to a column headed "Equivalent Soviet and American Cities in Mega-deaths."

The President pushed the book away and continued to speak to Premier Kissof. "What? Are you absolutely certain?... Well then, if the plane gets through we've had it! You're positive it's set to go off on ten megatons?" He sighed. "Okay, I guess we'll just have to keep our fingers crossed and concentrate on getting that plane."

He passed the phone to Staines, who covered the mouthpiece with his hand. Then he turned to General Turgidson. "Is there really a chance for that plane to get through?"

Turgidson looked quickly at the Russian Ambassador, breathed heavily, then said, "Mister President, if I can speak freely now, sir. The Russkie talks big, but frankly we think he's short of know-how. I mean you just can't take a bunch of ignorant peasants and expect them to understand a machine like one of our boys." He glanced again at De Sadeski. "And I don't mean that as an insult, Ambassador. Hell, we all know what kind of guts a Russkie has. Just look how many millions of them those Nazis killed, and hell, they still wouldn't quit."

The President said sharply, "General, stick to the point, please."

Turgidson was becoming excited now. This was a subject he knew. This was something on which he was an expert. "Well sir, if the pilot's really a good man, I mean really sharp, hell, he can barrel that plane along so low, well, I mean, you've just got to see it sometime. A real big plane like a fifty-two, its jet exhaust frying chickens in the barnyard…"

"Has he a chance?" the President cut in.

General Turgidson was now almost feverish with excitement. He said loudly, "Has he a chance? Hell, yes. He has one *hell* of a chance."

Turgidson looked round the table. As he saw the gloom on the faces of the men there, he realized suddenly the implications of what he had said.

The President looked at the displays, then said with quiet dignity, "Now wait a minute, wait a minute, I think I might just have an idea how to get the recall signal to them."

He picked up his phone. "Well, Dimitri, I guess you're just going to have to stop the plane. Dimitri, I'm sorry they're jamming your radar and flying low, but I mean, they're trained that way, you know. Look Dimitri, you know exactly where they're going and I'm sure your entire air defense can pull in a single plane…I…Dimitri, if our air staff says its primary target is Laputa and its secondary target is Borchav, you can believe it…well I mean, it's not going to help either one of us if the Doomsday Machine goes off, now is it?… Dimitri, there's absolutely no point in getting hysterical at a time like this. Will you listen to me, Dimitri? Dimitri, can I give you a word of advice? Dimitri, will you lis... Dimitri, can I give you...can I...Dimitri...Dimitri, can I give you a word of advice? Look, put everything you've got in those two sectors and you can't miss... Well, we'll keep our fingers crossed, and remember, Dimitri, we're all in this thing together. I mean, we're right behind you, Dimitri."

The President lit a cigarette as he listened to the Russian Premier. Then he said indignantly, "What do you mean, two months behind? Oh I see, you mean the cloud of radioactivity will reach us two months after you? You do? Well, Dimitri, I don't think that's a very nice thing to say... Well I know it wasn't a nice thing to *do*, but I didn't do it, Dimitri, it wasn't me... Dimitri, all right, so he *was* one of our generals... But this kind of attitude won't help either of us. Listen, Dimitri, I have been consulting one of my generals...no, *not* the general who sent them in, and he suggested something which gave me an idea... Well, do you want to hear it? It's a great idea. Now listen, Dimitri, as well as concentrating all the defenses you got on those two sectors, why don't you order your searchlights...you do have search-lights?... You do, well that's great, why not order all your searchlights to signal the recall code to the plane? They're bound to see it, and those boys are well trained. They'll turn back."

Doctor Strangelove looked thoughtfully at the President as he replaced the phone. He did not think those fools would ever succeed in destroying the last plane. He looked away and concentrated more than ever on his scheme to save at least a nucleus of specimens of the human race.

LEPER COLONY

King said, "Awright, she's flyin' an' I can hold her. Sweets, you remember when we were out with those crazy mixed-up fellas from Eight twenty-seven Bomb Wing?"

Sweets said, "Yeah, King, I remember."

"Now seems to me one of *their* targets was around this neighborhood."

"Yeah, that's right." He leaned forward. "I'll check the map."

"Check the fuel first," King said. "Gimme exactly how many air miles we got left."

Sweets said instantly, "I just checked, King. One hundred twenty as of now."

Beside him Lothar Zogg nodded silent agreement.

Sweets looked at the map, then said, "Got it right here. No name, just listed as Missile Complex Sixty-nine. That was the place, I'm sure."

"Range?"

Sweets said, "Ninety miles."

"Gimme a course.

"Two-eight-zero," Sweets said instantly. "Should take you right in."

"Two-eight-zero," King repeated, and leaned forward to adjust his gyros. He lifted the bomber over rising ground as he straightened from the turn.

Sweets said, "We've got easy ground between here and the target, King. Nothing above a few hundred feet."

"Awright," King said. "Here we go, boys."

Lothar Zogg said, "King, what if the Eight twenty-seven Bomb Wing already hit that target?"

"They won't," King said. "They're about six hours behind us. They'll probably decide to take out Laputa.

That answer you?"

"That answers me." Lothar looked in the locker under his table.

He took from it a thick folder and quickly riffled through the transparencies in it. He selected four of them and looked at them critically in the light of his radarscope. He said, "I got it."

King said, "Okay, Lothar."

Lothar Zogg fitted one of the transparencies to his scope. "Looks good, King. Nice clean picture."

King said, "Goldy, kin you get off a message sayin' we diverted to hit Missile Complex Sixty-nine?"

Goldberg said quickly, "I can't, King."

"Why in hell not?"

"Won't transmit, like I told you. Reason is the wiring's all gone."

"Okay," King said philosophically. "Don't matter much anyway. Lothar, get them bomb doors open when Sweets says we're eighty miles from target."

"Sure, King."

THE WAR ROOM

There was an atmosphere of gloom in the big room. Some people were sitting around the table, others were at the long table, listlessly picking at food from the dishes there.

The President lit another cigarette. He had already exceeded his quota, but he ignored this.

Staines said urgently, "Sir, Premier Kissof is on the line again."

The President quickly lifted his phone. He said, "Hello, Dimitri. You did what? How did that happen... Well, never mind, hold on a minute, will you?"

He covered the mouthpiece with his hand and said to General Turgidson, "They say they've lost the bomber."

Turgidson said, "Mister President, you don't surprise me. I told you that those boys low down would be mighty difficult to track."

The President said, "Hello, Dimitri, you still there?... Yes, well we knew it was going to be difficult, Dimitri, but there's still a chance... Come on now, Dimitri, there's still a chance."

On the Big Board the track predicted for *Leper Colony* continued on toward its primary target.

The President spoke into his phone again. "Dimitri, you there?"

Doctor Strangelove, his eyes gleaming, was busily making calculations on a scratch pad. He felt sure now that he had the answer. He multiplied and divided, added and subtracted, checked and rechecked, until he was certain his answer was correct.

As Strangelove worked, the President listened to Premier Kissof's voice and the translation. Then he said, "We've done all that, Dimitri. Please believe me. That is its target...sure they'll understand it if they see the code flashed at them...well of course I know, I have all my advisers round me now, and they're the best in the world... Well I'm sorry, Dimitri, I don't mean that exactly, but you know what I mean? All right, in America then, now don't let's fall out about small things now, Dimitri... All right, I'll wait for your news."

The President replaced his telephone and sat back in his seat. At this moment there was nothing more he could do.

LEPER COLONY

The wind blowing in through the many holes in *Leper Colony* chilled the flight deck with its icy blast.

But King was sweating, both because of the physical effort needed to control the heavy bomber so close to the deck, and the concentration needed to take them successfully to their target.

He lifted the bomber gently over a high incline, then let down to the deck again. His flying was smooth and precise, the flying of a man absolutely determined he would reach his target.

Sweets Kivel said, 'We're right on track, King. E.T.A. about nine minutes. You have a clear run now, nothing above one hundred feet."

"That's great," King said. "We're gonna make it, fellas."

Sweets said, "We got fuel for twelve minutes."

"Roger."

King considered exactly what he should do. He was thinking about this when Lothar Zogg broke in.

Lothar Zogg said, "Major Kong."

"Yeah?"

"There's something wrong with the bomb-bay doors."

"What are you talkin' about?"

"They're stuck tight. I can't get 'em open."

"What?"

"They must be damaged."

"That's impossible!"

"I've tried everything. But the bomb-door warning light keeps flashing."

"Lieutenant Zogg, if this is some kind of a trick, you'll spend the rest of your life in a federal prison!"

"Major, I've tried everything, including emergency power."

"You open them doors! You hear me?"

"I can't! Why don't you come down and see for your-self?"

King said sharply, "Dietrich!"

Dietrich came forward. He said, "What's up?"

"You think you can keep this on two-eight-zero and not clip any treetops?"

"Sure thing."

Dietrich slid into King's seat and took over. He had received enough training as copilot to fly the bomber while it was airborne. He could not have taken off or landed; but he could keep it flying in an emergency. He looked ahead anxiously as King went down the compartment hatch.

King arrived in the bomb-navigator section of the lower deck. He said, "Let's see."

Lothar looked up at him and moved to the left to let King see the equipment. He said, "Try it yourself."

King flipped the switches controlling the bomb doors. The lights indicated a negative response.

King looked round the lower deck. He saw a fire hatchet clipped to the side of the bomber and grabbed it. Then he kicked open a small door in the rear of the section.

He said, "I'm goin' down there."

Lothar Zogg said, "That's dangerous, King. If those doors open you're liable to fall out."

"That's right, an' I guess that's a chance I got to take."

THE WAR ROOM

General Turgidson's phone sounded. He picked it up. He listened, then said abruptly, "I told you not to call me at this number."

He heard Miss Foreign Affairs saying, "I'm sorry, Buck, but are you going to be much longer?"

"I don't know."

"Well," she said, "what do you want me to do?"

Turgidson looked around the table. He did not think any one was watching him. He said quietly, "Watch television."

Miss Foreign Affairs said plaintively, "But, Buck, the late late show has been over for hours...you know, Buck, I don't think you really love me at all, I don't think you miss me at all. I don't think you respect me either... No you don't, it's just physical."

Turgidson breathed heavily, and said, "Now look, baby, I've told you not to call me here...and it isn't just physical. No, it is *not*! Goddammit, it's not just physical, kitten. Now go watch television."

He slammed the phone down and smiled at the President, who was watching the Big Board.

LEPER COLONY

Major King Kong slid open the trap door and dropped to the floor of the vast bomb bay. The two bombs, *Lolita* and *Hi-There*, were taller than he, though they were lying horizontally.

King chopped at the bomb doors with his hatchet, chopped at the locks and hinges, stamped on the doors, and kicked and beat them, trying to force them loose. But they were tightly shut.

He swept his arm across his forehead to remove the sweat which was trickling down into his eyes. His vision cleared, and in front of him he saw the sign which read: NUCLEAR WARHEADS. HANDLE WITH CARE.

He tried again to force the doors loose, but they refused to open.

Lothar Zogg, looking down into the bomb bay, said, "King?"

"I'm awright," King said irritably. "But these bomb doors are stuck tighter than Dick's hatband." He began to climb the ladder, then turned back to the bombs and patted both of them affectionately.

He said, "Don't worry, ole buddies. You'll make it."

Lothar helped him up to the cabin.

King said, "Thanks, Lothar."

Lothar Zogg beamed and said, "That's okay, King."

King patted Lothar on the shoulder and moved up and forward to the flight deck.

Dietrich pulled back on the controls and took the bomber three hundred feet higher as he made room for King. He said, "Everything's okay, King."

King slid in the seat, and checked the instruments rapidly. He said, "Sweets, how long till we hit the primary?"

"Six minutes."

"Okay," King said. "Dietrich, you come on up here."

THE WAR ROOM

The President said, "Who was that, Buck?" Turgidson smiled, "Well now, Mister President, you know, all kinds of zany phone calls come in here. Ought to make it an unlisted number if you ask me."

Turgidson's phone sounded. He grabbed it, conscious that the President was watching him.

He said, "No...no...well of course I know that... Look, I just can't talk now...my President needs me... well, who do you think I mean? Sure, the President of the United States... Of course he is. So goodbye."

He replaced the phone.

The President looked at him coldly. "Good news, Buck?" he asked.

Turgidson said, "Well, kind of medium, Mister President."

LEPER COLONY

King picked up the triptych of fierce-looking warriors and studied it. He held it close to him and said, "Don't you worry, ole buddies." Then he let the triptych swing back against the instrument board and said, "Lieutenant Zogg, arm the bombs for impact."

"Arm them for impact?"

"That's right. You set them bombs for impact, you hear?"

"But we can't get the bomb doors open."

"Lieutenant Zogg, I've given you an order. Arm them bombs for impact!"

Lothar Zogg said patiently, "But, King, they're *already* armed for impact."

Major Kong said, after considering Lothar's remarks, "Awright, Lothar, awright, awright. I gotta lot to think about, don't fergit that."

"I'm not forgetting it, King."

"Awright, so shut up an' let me concentrate."

Lothar lapsed into offended silence.

King said, "Sweets, how far are we from target?"

Kivel replied immediately, "Four minutes."

King said, "Okay, I'm goin' down to them bomb doors again. Got an idea I mebbe can open them."

THE WAR ROOM

The President said, "No contact, Staines?"

Staines said, "No contact, sir."

The President sighed. "You'd think their whole air defense could intercept one bomber."

Turgidson said, "Well now, sir, it's not that easy. You got to remember that plane's real low. Can't get radar response at that height."

Everyone heard Turgidson's speech. They looked at the Big Board.

The Russian bomber threat was still building up over the Arctic.

LEPER COLONY

King pulled back on the controls and the bomber started climbing.

Dietrich moved forward and tapped King on the shoulder.

King turned his head. He said, "Okay, Dietrich, now you take her up to ten thousand while I go down to them bomb doors. You understand me?"

Dietrich said, "Sure, King."

"And once she's at ten thousand you level her out, okay?"

"Okay, King."

Dietrich settled himself in the seat and concentrated.

King moved toward the rear of the bomber and disappeared down the steps to the bomb-navigator compartment.

Sweets said, "Well hi, King, what you doing down here?"

King ignored him. He said, "Lothar, you know this happened to me once before?"

"No, I didn't know, King."

"Well it did," King said, "an' we put it right. You know that?"

"No, I didn't know it, King." Lothar's voice was apologetic.

"Well you know it now," King said irritably. "You just help me down that goddam pipe."

Lothar moved forward immediately. He said, "Sure, King, I'll help you."

"An' you put those bomb-door switches to positive, you understand?"

"Sure, King, I understand."

King descended into the bomb bay for the second

time. He had remembered how once the mechanism controlling the bomb doors had been affected by a broken wire. It was possible, he thought, that the same thing had happened.

He quickly inspected the wiring in the roof of the bomb bay. He thought he saw the connection that had been broken. He patted *Hi-There* affectionately, then climbed onto *Lolita*. It was a difficult climb. He stood on *Lolita* and reached for the broken wires, connected them, then sat down on *Lolita* to throw the emergency switches on the side of the bomber.

Lothar Zogg looked down at him anxiously. He said, "You all right, King?"

"Sure," King said. "I'm awright."

He was sitting astride *Lolita*, ready to throw the final switch. He looked carefully at his watch. He estimated they were over their target. He reached across and threw the switch.

Nobody would ever know what passed through King's mind in the next few seconds. The bomb doors began to open and King was illuminated by the light from below.

Lolita began to fall and King fell with her. Perhaps he thought in this ultimate moment that he could accelerate the bomb's fall, or maybe even give it guidance. Nobody knows.

King dropped with the bomb from *Leper Colony*. What happened after that is anybody's guess.

What is certain is that three minutes later *Lolita* detonated in a twenty-megaton explosion.

THE DOOMSDAY MACHINE

Under the perpetually fog-shrouded mountain in the empty arctic wastes of northern Siberia, seismographs, radio antennae, and computers analyzed the material they had received.

The memory banks clicked as they examined it.

They arrived at their decision.

For a few seconds there was silence.

Then there was an explosion that made the bomb from *Leper Colony* look like kids' firecrackers.

And billions of tons of earth and debris rose into the air to begin their lethal journey around the globe.

THE WAR ROOM

The President put down his phone. He said, "In spite of all our efforts, gentlemen, in spite of all we've done, they've delivered their bomb. And apparently the Soviet bomb has detonated in retaliation. There it is. The Doomsday Machine has been triggered! God knows it's not our fault."

General Turgidson said, "It's wrong." He sighed, then said, "Totally wrong."

Admiral Randolph also shook his head. He said, "It isn't *right*."

They were not really talking to each other. In fact everyone was walking round talking to himself.

General Turgidson said, "I don't care what anyone says, it just doesn't seem to make sense to end all human life on Earth."

Admiral Randolph said, "It's *wrong*."

General Faceman said, "It's not right."

General Turgidson said, "It isn't *right*."

Admiral Randolph said thoughtfully, "I suppose the fishes will be okay—at least some of them."

"Ugh-hhh, that's a horrible thought." This was a comment from General Faceman.

General Turgidson said bitterly, "It's all so pointless. I mean, a man works his whole life fighting for something, and this is what he gets. You know, I can see twenty, forty, a hundred million dead, but everybody? It's just a damned shame, and I don't mind saying so."

Staines turned to the President, "Mister President, how are we going to break this to the people? I mean, it's going to do one hell of a thing to your image."

The President irritably shrugged off Staines's question. He said, "Mister Ambassador, how much time have we got?"

The Ambassador's voice was weary. "Four—possibly six months in the Northern Hemisphere. Perhaps a year in the southern latitudes."

"Perhaps *not!*"

Everyone turned to the man who had spoken so emphatically.

It was Doctor Strangelove.

The President said, "What do you mean, Doctor Strangelove?"

"Mister President, I would not rule out the chance to preserve a nucleus of human specimens."

The President looked at him. "You mean there's a way? There's a way to do this?"

Doctor Strangelove moved his wheelchair back from the table. He was excited and again his right arm was jerking spasmodically. He said to the President, "There is."

"How?"

"At the bottom of some of our deeper mine shafts."

"At the bottom of mines? I don't get you, I don't get you at all."

"It's easy."

Turgidson turned to his aide. He said, "What the hell is this guy talking about?"

Doctor Strangelove said, "I repeat, Mister President, I would *not* rule out the chance of preserving a nucleus of human specimens."

The President said wearily, "Doctor Strangelove, do you think you could possibly explain?"

"Of course."

"Then please do," the President said. He used his inhaler.

Doctor Strangelove leaned forward enthusiastically. He said, "Mister President, you are aware of the basic facts concerning radiation and human life?"

The President put his inhaler down on the table. He said, "Of course I am."

"So you can see, it's simple."

"What's simple?" the President snapped.

"The chance to preserve a nucleus of human specimens."

"You've already said that!"

"Yes," Doctor Strangelove said, "and, Mister President, I meant it."

"Goddammit!" The President exploded. "Just what do you mean?"

"Mine shafts."

"*What about mine shafts?*"

Doctor Strangelove said, "Oh, I thought you were with me, Mister President."

"I am with you. What about mine shafts?"

Strangelove said, "Mine shafts? Why, the chance to preserve a nucleus of human specimens."

The President drummed his fingers on the table and looked at Strangelove.

Doctor Strangelove smiled at him happily. He moved his chair closer to the President, conscious that everyone in the room was watching him. He did not object to this, indeed he found it gratifying. When his chair stopped near the President he said, "Well look, Mister President, I'll explain."

The President said faintly, "Please."

"Of course! The radioactivity would not penetrate a mine thousands of feet deep."

The President looked at him blankly.

"In a matter of weeks sufficient improvements for dwelling space could be provided."

"You mean people would stay in there for almost a hundred years? Impossible."

Doctor Strangelove smiled tolerantly. As he spoke he gestured with his gloved right hand. "Mister President, man is an amazingly adaptable creature. After all, the conditions would be far superior to those of the *so-called* concentration camps, where there is ample evidence most of the wretched creatures clung desperately to life."

The President seemed unconvinced, but around the table it was apparent that Strangelove's proposal had not fallen upon deaf ears.

The President said, "How?"

MISSILE COMPLEX 69

Nothing remained of Missile Complex 69 or of Major King Kong.

He had hit his target and destroyed it. Now the particles which had made him a human being rose into the atmosphere to add their small contribution to the radioactive particles from the explosion of the Doomsday Machine.

THE WAR ROOM

Doctor Strangelove smiled. He said, "It would not be difficult. Nuclear reactors could provide power almost indefinitely. Greenhouses could maintain plant life. Oxygen of course can be supplied by selected plants. This would enable an efficient filtration system to be installed in the shaft. Animals could be bred and slaughtered. A quick survey would have to be taken of all the suitable mine sites in the country, but I shouldn't be surprised if space for several hundred thousand of our people could be prepared."

The President said thoughtfully, "But only several hundred thousand saved. There would be panic, rioting, absolute chaos."

Strangelove said, "I am sure the armed forces could deal with any disobedience. Men cannot fight against tanks and machine guns, Mister President. This we have proved."

President Muffley shook his head. "But to take such a decision...who would choose the survivors?"

Strangelove said, "A special committee would have to be appointed to study and recommend the method and criteria of choice."

The President observed the jerking of Strangelove's right arm. Naturally he knew everything about Strangelove's personal history. He knew also that Strangelove was sometimes erratic. But he had contributed a large amount to the defense of the country. He said, "How could anyone decide a thing like that?"

Strangelove said, "Offhand, I should say that in addition to the factors of youth, health, sexual fertility, intelligence, and a cross section of necessary skills, it would be *absolutely vital that our top government and military men* be included, to foster and impart the required principles of leadership and tradition."

The arrow had not missed its mark, and around the table there was an outbreak of sober, nodding heads. Attention was concentrated more than ever on Doctor Strangelove.

Strangelove went on. "Naturally they would breed prodigiously, eh? There would be much time and little to do. With the proper breeding techniques, and starting with a ratio of, say, ten women to each man, I should estimate the progeny of the original group of two hundred thousand would emerge a hundred years later as well over a hundred million. Naturally the group would have to engage in enlarging the original living space. This would have to be continuous. They would have to do it so long as they stayed in the mine shaft."

General Turgidson said quietly to his aide, "You know, I'm beginning to think this Kraut has really got something."

The President said, "How long would that be? What will there be left when they emerge?"

Strangelove said, "When they emerge a good deal of present real estate and machine tools will still be recoverable, if they are moth-balled in advance. I suggest this should be put in hand immediately. I guess they could then work their way back to our present gross national product inside twenty years."

The President said, "But look here, Strangelove, won't this, er, nucleus of survivors be so shocked, grief-stricken, and anguished that they will envy the dead and not wish to go on living?"

"Certainly not, sir. When they go down into the mine, everyone else will still be alive. They will have no shocking memories, and the prevailing emotion should be one of nostalgia for those left behind, combined with a spirit of bold curiosity for the adventure ahead. This will, I think, encourage them."

General Turgidson looked at Strangelove. He said, "You mentioned the ratio of ten women to each man. Wouldn't that necessitate abandoning the so-called monogamous form of sexual relationship—at least so far as men are concerned?"

"Regrettably, yes. But it is a sacrifice required for the future of the human race. I hasten to add that, since each man will be required to perform prodigious service along those lines, the women will have to be selected for their sexual characteristics, which will have to be of a highly stimulating order."

The Russian Ambassador, De Sadeski, said enthusiastically, "Strangelove, I must confess you have an astonishingly good idea there."

"Thank you, sir."

General Turgidson said, "Mister President?"

"Yes, General Turgidson."

"Mister President, I think we've got to look into this thing from the military point of view. I mean, if the Russkies stashed away some big bombs and we didn't, when they come out in a hundred years, they could take over."

General Faceman broke into the conversation. "I agree, Mister President. In fact they might even try an immediate sneak attack so they could take over our mine-shaft space."

General Turgidson said, "I think we would be extremely naïve, Mister President, to imagine that these new developments will affect the Soviet expansionist policy. We must be increasingly on the alert for their moves to take over other mine-shaft space in order to breed more prodigiously than us, and so knock us out through superior numbers when we emerge."

"Us, General Turgidson?"

Turgidson said loudly, "Mister President, *we must not allow a mine-shaft gap!*"

EPILOGUE

Though the little-known planet Earth, remotely situated in another galaxy, is admittedly of mere academic interest to us today, we have presented this quaint comedy of galactic pre-history as another in our series, *The Dead Worlds of Antiquity*.

AFTER HOURS

Edwin Torres

The classic 70s New York street novel

"An authentic original…awesomely energetic…a joy to read" LOS ANGELES TIMES

Older and wiser after five years inside, Carlito Brigante, Puerto Rican heavy hitter and drug dealer is looking to slow down, maybe even get out. But as a name with a rep to uphold it's tough. Everything's changed, it's the late 70s and the heroin has been replaced by coke and the disco scene is in full flow. Carlito needs to pull in money somehow so he buys into an after-hours club in Harlem while he works on the right move to make. Meanwhile, Dave Kleinfeld, the lawyer who sprung Carlito from the Federal Pen, turns out to be up to his neck in it with the Mafia and wants to call in a favor, and as Carlito says "a favor can kill faster than a bullet".

Carlito's Way and *After Hours* were filmed by Brian de Palma in 1993 as *Carlito's Way* starring Al Pacino.

1-85375-338-6
£6.99

BUTTERFIELD 8

John O'Hara

with a new introduction by MATTHEW J BRUCCOLI

"a great social realist" VILLAGE VOICE

Set amid Manhattan's fast set in the early 1930s, *Butterfield 8* is the tale of a sexual encounter between a married society man and a tragically corrupted young woman, that tears both their worlds apart. Told from a number of perspectives it shows Manhattan in a state of turmoil – a society where the Crash and Prohibition have left the old certainties in tatters, vividly capturing the beautiful and damned of the speakeasy crowd. It is one of the finest works by one of the greatest American novelists of the century.

Butterfield 8 was filmed in 1960, starring Laurence Harvey, Eddie Fisher and Elizabeth Taylor in an Oscar-winning role as Gloria.

1-85375-319-X
£5.99

SHOOT THE PIANO PLAYER

David Goodis

with a new introduction by GEOFFREY O'BRIEN

"Goodis's fiction contains a tortured beauty that can take the breath away" WOODY HAUT

Eddie plays to forget. Haunted by his past, he hides from life playing nightly in a skid row drinking joint – a world of hookers, lowlifes and petty crooks. A hopeless ghost of a man who has ceased caring about himself, he saves his loyalty for others: his fellow lowlife damned, his undeserving, no-good family and the waitress who momentarily takes him away from it all. And it is this loyalty that eventually drags him down in this blackest of noir tales.

Adapted for the screen by Francois Truffaut in 1960, *Tirez sur le Pianiste* is seen as one of the key films of the French Nouvelle Vague.

1-85375-308-4
£5.99

THIEVES LIKE US

Edward Anderson

"One of the great forgotten novels of the thirties"
RAYMOND CHANDLER

Somewhere between the hardboiled talk of Dashiell
Hammett and the dustbowl poetry of John Steinbeck lies
the doomed romanticism of Edward Anderson's *Thieves
Like Us*. When three small-time country gangsters break jail,
they return like moths to a flame to the only life they know
– small-town bank-robbing. And when the youngest of
them falls in love with one of the older gangster's cousins it
becomes a classic tale of love on the run with nowhere to
hide and no hope of reprieve.

First published in 1939, *Thieves Like Us* was powerfully
adapted for the screen by Nicholas Ray in 1948 as
They Live By Night and once again under its original title
by Robert Altman in 1973.

1-85375-311-4
£5.99